TASHA'S GOT A BABY

S. YVONNE

❀ Created with Vellum

CHAPTER 1 'YEAR OF 2000'

"*T*asha… Tasha come on." Pepper whispered through the window of the roach infested apartment while she stayed on the lookout. She shivered wearing her bomber since it was cold as hell outside but after being out there standing around trash and crack heads for the past thirty minutes she was ready to go and she knew Tasha should've been done. The window was rusted around the edges and the windowpane itself was fucked up but Pepper was careful not to touch it cause she didn't want to cut herself.

The only thing she was able to get a good visual of was the dirty air mattress on the floor that Tasha and QUA used whenever they were getting busy but today it wasn't QUA… it was Officer Moron's bitch ass cause that's exactly what both Tasha and Pepper called him. Pepper couldn't stand him especially cause he was blackmailing Tasha into doing what he wanted her to do and he had a whole wife and little ass kids at home. For whatever reason though, he just couldn't stay away from Tasha.

A few minutes later he came walking out in full uniform zipping up his pants making his way to his patrol car that sat waiting for him. Pepper gawked his way as she ignored him... she read the words on his vehicle 'City of Miami Police'... she shook her head watching him pull off. It wasn't even that Officer Moron was a bad person... he was just a fucked up nigga in a uniform that's all. Coming from a crack infested neighborhood like the one that Pepper and Tasha lived in... he knew those kids did anything to survive whether it was selling drugs, or selling ass and if they needed to hustle with a peace of mind and not worry about getting busted then they had to do what he said in order to make the bread.

"Let me get a honey bun..." A rusted crack head sluggishly walked up to Pepper trying to hand her some change from his ashy hands for some dope. Spit flew from his mouth as he spoke to her, which was a result from missing half his teeth. Pepper took a step back and frowned just as Tasha rounded the corner.

"Nah... step the fuck off." She slapped his hand away.

The sun was setting causing an orange and reddish color hue above them, but down on the bottom in the real world... everything was black and white for them, sometimes even grey. That's how shit was. "Here..." Tasha passed Pepper a fifty-dollar bill and stuffed the rest in her pocket as they casually walked off like nothing happened. "I'm sick of this shit... on God. I'm tired of fucking that old ass nigga. I don't understand why he just won't leave me alone."

"You know why." Pepper suggested. "You hugging the block all day and night, you're a runner, and you in and out of stores all day..."

Tasha held up a hand... "Yeah.... I get it. I gotta take care of myself though." She looked up when they reached their building. Kids were running everywhere, cracked up glass was scattered, the walls wore graffiti from different gangs, dope boys hugged the corners and so on and so on. From the top stoop, they heard the sounds of music playing. She dreaded going inside the apartment that she shared with her family. They were all in a 3-bedroom apartment... all 9 of them. Tasha, her mama, her mama's boyfriend, her cousin DayDay, his twin brother RayRay, DayDay's lil son Darius, her brothers Eli and Cleo, and her niece Summer with whom she shared a room. Everybody else had to just figure it out. "You just better be glad he don't fuck with you." Tasha told Pepper.

"They don't call me Pepper for no reason. I'm black as the dirt what the fuck he want with me." She looked herself over. Pepper was a short 5'3 in height with skin as dark as the night sky but she was pretty with a decent shape. Tasha on the other hand was just like Pepper; an around the way girl... golden brown skin, same height, round face and chinky eyes. She wasn't all that thick but she was exactly what a 16 year old was supposed to be. They both wore huge gold earrings and Cuban link chains compliments of the dope boys that were crushing on them. Unlike Tasha... Pepper wasn't a hustler, she wasn't built like Tasha; Tasha knew how to sale drugs and pop tags off of clothes but Pepper was too scary for that. Most of the time Tasha just looked out for her.

Snapping from her thoughts, Tasha looked at Pepper and frowned. "Just cause you black don't mean you ain't pretty. Who the fuck ever told you some shit like that? That's weak as hell."

"That's what Officer Moron said... plenty of times."

Tasha's stomach did flips thinking about how she had to constantly lay there while he pumped in and out of her until he was done on their once a week meetings. She regretted day by day ever getting into the car with him three months ago to 'take a ride' and she only went cause she was caught red handed selling a bomb. The rent was due and nobody in her apartment had it so she had to miss school for a week to

3

make the money. Officer Moron, whose real name is Officer Ralph pulled up on her in the middle of a transaction and from that day forward she had to fuck him in order to keep him from turning her in and she wasn't trying to go to juvi.

"Fuck him... he would be fine as hell if he wasn't a pervert." Tasha sighed.

"Yo Tasha!

Her and both Pepper spun around. QUA was walking up on them with a mug on his face. Skin brown like a chestnut with a mouth full of gold teeth, medium built, dimples, low fade with the perfect waves in his head with a fresh tape. He wore a simple black bomber, chain around his neck, a pair of Jordan's and some black baggy jeans. He was two years older than them both but was a hot head and always trying to run Tasha and keep tabs on her. She loved QUA but she knew she was too young to be letting a nigga beat on her. Knowing that he was mad about her not answering her phone she was prepared to take off running but he grabbed her roughly by the arm before she could. "Let me go!" She tried to yank away.

"Nah." He growled. "Where the fuck you been?" He asked her with balled up lips like one wrong move and he was gonna hit her ass. Pepper wanted to break it up but she had learned long ago with these two to stay out of their shit cause nine times outta ten they ass's were gonna make up and she was still gonna be mad, *'but still, he better not had hit her though'* Pepper thought to herself with her arms crossed.

"QUA! I wasn't doing nothinggggg." Tasha whined trying to get away. It was an ongoing circus with the two of them; a real love-hate relationship but no matter what they always had each other's back.

"Stop lying! You always fucking lying yo! You smell like a whole nigga!" He barked with his other fist balled up. It wasn't that QUA didn't love Tasha... he just didn't trust her and if she thought she was gonna play with his heart she had him fucked up. Tasha couldn't even believe he was coming like this as much as he cheated. If it was ten girls in the park he probably fucked seven of them. Tasha had numerous of fights around the hood cause of him and every time she won. She hadn't run across not one person yet who could beat her ass.

With panic in her voice she knew she was about to get hit so she did what she knew to do. With all her strength she raised her knee catching him right in the balls causing him to let go and bend over in pain holding himself. Pepper and Tasha both gave each other a knowing look before they took off running separate ways to their buildings and she knew she was going to have to hide out for a few days. Tasha managed to make it inside safe but she was out of breath and her tiny apartment was in an uproar. Everybody was in the living room. DayDay and RayRay sat at the table breaking down some weed. Her mama Vashon stood over the stove smoking a cigarette and frying some chicken while everybody else watched television.

Two-year old Summer grabbed a piece of the weed from the table ready to put it in her mouth but Tasha caught her in time gently picking her up. "Summer... that's a no no okay? No-No." She told her carrying her into her room. "Ya'll stupid ass people can't even watch the damn baby!" She slammed the door of her room and sat Summer on the bed turning on some cartoons. Summer should've been sleep by now. Tasha's room was only but so big. She had a little twin bed pushed up against the wall; and a nightstand, a lamp and a dresser that held her clothes. She didn't have anything hung up in her closet; instead she had her valuable shit in a suitcase that she kept a lock on cause her shit had come up missing way too many times.

Removing the money from her pocket she peeled off two

hundred and sat in on the dresser knowing that her mother was coming for it. Next, she peeled off her clothes and show-ered coming out fully dressed in something different, a complete fleece suit with a hoodie and a pair of Nikes. Summer was good and sleeping so she tucked the toddler under the covers but left the television on. In the top of her closet she stood on her tippy toes ruffling through the box at the top that she was looking for. When she opened it up, she pulled out the Ziploc bags filled with crack and then another one with some coke before tucking it inside of her jacket.

Tasha made sure she looked both ways before she crossed over to the next building not wanting to run into QUA, and she made sure to put his ass on call block too cause if she didn't give him at least a few days to calm down she knew she was gon' have to fight his ass. Her Nike's hit the pave-ment when she jumped down the steps of the shallow hall-ways that hid behind a wall where she sat with her hands tucked waiting to hear a knock on the wall. When she heard it, she would open up the makeshift hole that had a piece of wood covering it and make her serve knowing this was gon' be a long ass night since it's the first of the month.

CHAPTER 2

(A couple hours later)

It was booming all night and when Tasha realized that she was almost out of work it was time to get ready to go. What most people didn't know about Tasha was that she had a beautiful voice. A voice that sounded like heaven on earth and most nights she'd sit and hum to herself or sing a low melody knowing that her situation would change soon. She placed her hoodie over her head and tucked her phone in her pocket getting ready to walk away only to be stopped by a knocking. "The fuck?" She mumbled. "What?"

"Sing again" a low raspy voice whispered behind the wall. A voice that sounded all too familiar to her, it was the same crack-head who never had money to buy shit from her but always wanted her to sing. "Sing again."

With her brows furrowed and her face balled up Tasha sucked her teeth, "Fuck outta here this ain't no free show." She spat and ran off. She didn't know why she ran, she just did cause it made her feel better; that and she also didn't like to walk through the projects in the wee hours of the morning risking getting shot up or shot at from somebody tryna rob her cause now days they'd rob a toddler for a tricycle, so she knew damn well they didn't care about her. The wind smacked her face as she ran but when she made it to her door she was relieved. As soon as she stuck her key in the door, she locked it back and removed her hoodie from her head.

"Where the fuck you been Tasha?" A smooth voice asked from the couch causing her to jump. It was dark but she was able to see the smoke and smell the cigarette.

"I was out." She mumbled to her mother and slowly walked away.

"I want my house locked down at a certain hour Tasha! And if you can't handle the rules then you can get the fuck out." She said cool like before blowing a cloud of smoke from her mouth. "Your fast ass-think you grown. Gon' fuck around and end up pregnant and I'm not taking care of your fucking baby while you out fucking all night." Tasha lowered her head piercing her lips together and sucked her teeth loud enough for her mama to hear. Not even a second later a coffee mug came flying toward her causing her to duck in the nick of time and behind her the loud thud and the crashing of the mug hitting the wall could be heard. "Now keep talking back!" Her mama warned her.

Tasha, whom never listened, rambled on. "How the hell am I supposed to get money then if I don't stay out late ma? Ya'll some hypocrites!" She openly spoke her mind and slammed her room door. Behind closed doors she paced the room wanting to scream as she dropped all the money from the night on the bed. "I'm sick of this shit yo! How the fuck I'm supposed to get money? How the fuck am I supposed to pay my portion of the rent if I don't fucking work? How the fuck I'ma take care of myself? Ouuuu I fucking hate her yo! I hate my fucking life!" She slapped her hands on her thighs and flopped on the edge of the bed as the perspiration built up on her forehead. She took slow, deep breaths before peeling her clothes off and throwing on an oversized shirt. She had two hours left before she had to get to school.

The blaring sound of the alarm coming from her phone woke her up a couple of hours later. Taking a deep breath, she exhaled her morning breath and then wiped the crust from the cracks of her eyes before heading to brush her teeth and take a quick shower. There was a 2 minute rule in their apartment cause it was way too many people who needed to shower and in order to preserve the hot water they had to do everything they needed to do in two minutes. She was in and out like the lightning and once she dressed in a Wilson outfit, she threw on her bamboo earrings and some lip-gloss before locking up her suitcase and securing the key around her wrist. She made sure she stuffed her money, fixed Summer a bowl of cereal and left her at the table to eat it when she bounced. Making her way through the halls she thought she was in the clear when her feet hit the outside pavement but she wasn't as lucky as she thought cause QUA was lingering on the stoop and as soon as her saw her, he snatched her ass up.

He looked much calmer than the previous day so she relaxed a little but she still tried to remove his hands from the way he had her helmed up against the wall. Her eyes roamed her surroundings hoping that someone would notice them. "Hey...hey... QUA." She spoke to him nervous like. "You know, you're too fine to be so mad all the time." She tried to soften up with him.

With a glaring look in his eyes, to a blind man you could see that he was simply just young and in love. Not even he knew how to deal with his feelings cause sometimes Tasha was just too much for him, he didn't understand why she was in such a rush to grow up so fast or why she kept all the shit under her roof a secret. One of the main reasons he didn't trust her. "Tasha, I'm not fucking playin' wit' you right now yo. That's yo problem you play too fuckin' much. You think my feelings something to play wit'? Cause if so we can end this shit now." He suggested.

She felt bad knowing that she was truly hurting him with all her secrets but she felt as if she wasn't in a position to be telling him the truth about how she's really surviving out here. He knew about the drugs but he knew nothing about the sex and she prayed he didn't find out cause whether he knew it or not, he was her first true love. "I can't see myself without you QUA. What I'mma do if you leave me?" She found herself panicking as she dropped her eyes. From the corner she saw Officer Ralph turning the corner and looking right in their direction. QUA was getting ready to address her but before he could she had to do something quick. Although he had her helmed up she pulled him in close for a kiss until Officer Ralph passed by.

Caught up in her tongue circus QUA forgot why he was really mad that quick. Looking lovingly into her eyes he removed his hand and grabbed her hand rushing off. "Come on!" He led the way.

Tasha tried to use her weight to stay in the same spot while gently jerking back. "UN UN where we going? I have to go to schoollll." She whined. In reality she didn't give a fuck about school. She just didn't want to fuck him knowing that she had to fuck Officer Ralph the day before. She fo'sho felt like a low down little whore. Her pussy was still sore.

QUA casually placed her hand on his dick print through his pants with his eyes budging. "Yo Tasha, you see how hard you done got my dick? You gone have to make this right before we split ways today." He looked at her sideways. "You know you been real salty lately? You sure you not fucking nobody?" He flared his nostrils and tried to control his breathing. Even imagining something like that made him want to haul off and punch her ass.

After carefully weighing her options, she realized she didn't have a choice. She sucked up the tears in her eyes and followed him to 'the spot' the same exact spot that Officer Ralph fucked her in. When they made it inside, Tasha felt her stomach doing flips staring down at the mattress but she refused to lay down there. From behind, she felt QUA breathing on the nape of her neck while his hands slowly roamed her body. Tasha loved the feel of him, because her young heart loved him, but she was just scared. Being young teenagers she knew they knew nothing about the real foundation of sex, they only did it cause it felt good, but she wasn't even sure that she knew what a real orgasm even felt like.

Turning around, she wrapped her arms around his neck and kissed his lips vowing to make this quick and in no time they were naked while QUA stood behind her plummeting in and out of her silky opening as he rabbit fucked her into a frenzy until he was cumming all inside of her and she thanked God she was on the pill, which she always brought her packs hot off the streets since her mama never gave a damn about making her any kind of appointments. They were both exhausted after that but she knew they had to go, they both had to go to school. QUA fell back on the mattress after he was dressed staring at Tasha while she got dressed. "Let's just skip today, fuck it." He suggested.

"Nah" Tasha shook her head left to right without looking at him. She slipped her shoes back on and grabbed her stuff before looking to him. "I can't do that today. I gotta stop skipping school QUA, and you should too. It's two ways I'mma find my way outta of this slum and that's with my voice or my education cause I gotta get the fuck up outta here." She sighed and took a deep breath. "Look at our surroundings QUA... this shit is fucked up. This ain't no way to live. We're kids and we practically take care of our damn selves." Technically QUA was already 18, but to Tasha that was still a kid.

QUA lay there in deep thought himself and he promised if he ever made it out he was gonna take care of Tasha and marry her and make sure they was straight forever. He cared nothing about those other girls he fucked with cause Tasha is the only one that had his heart. He heard the cracking of her voice and felt bad... "Come here." He raised his arms up for her to come down to him and hug him.

Tasha wiped her eyes and sniffed. "Nah, I'm good."

"I said come here!" He growled causing her to scramble to him where she hugged him and lye her head on his chest not wanting to trigger his anger. QUA placed soft kisses all over her forehead. "It's gon' be aiight... we gon' get outta here one day." He assured her visualizing a near future of both of them being young, successful, married with some kids and all that.

"QUA..." Tasha whispered without looking up noticing that he'd been silent for a few minutes. "You sleep?" She asked.

"Nah..." He sighed.

She decided to use that opportunity to speak her mind. "You gotta really control your temper."

"I know man, shit I be trying to control the shit... but you make me so mad Tasha... like nobody makes me mad like you do cause you stay lying to a nigga. Like now, who's calling yo phone cause this the third time it done rang and you ignored it."

Tasha felt a lump in her throat forming cause she knew who it was... and she didn't want to answer but she could've beat her own ass for not putting the phone on vibrate either. She slowly got up and grabbed her things. "It's nobody obviously."

QUA casually got up and grabbed his shit. "That's the shit I be talking about! Let me get outta here before I fuckin' snap." Tasha tried to gently grab his shoulder from behind to stop him but he yanked away from her. "Don't touch me!"

"QUA wait! Don't go!" She ran behind him but he kept going while still yanking away. Tasha wouldn't let up, which pissed him off even more. Turning around he forcefully grabbed her by both arms and pushed her hard up against the wall where she looked terrified. She knew it wasn't right to keep lying to him but she just couldn't tell the truth, about nothing... nothing at all.

He stared at her with disappointment trying to control his breathing. "What Tasha? What man?"

She dropped her eyes. "Nothing... fuck it."

"Yeah... fuck it, cause I'm tired of you playin' these bitch ass games with me."

With that, he released his tight grip on her and let her go before leaving her there alone. Tasha felt like shit as she went down her call log erasing numbers with trembling hands. Before she walked out she had to get herself together while ignoring the aching in her arms. She knew Pepper was at the playground on the bench waiting for her. "Yo, where the fuck you been?" Pepper hopped off the bench when she spotted Tasha rounding the corner. She looked at her watch. "We about to be late."

"I know, my bad, come on." Tasha told her walking ahead. Pepper had to catch up to her to talk and as usual she was always cheery and hyped up while fast-talking. "Ouu bitch you lucky cause QUA was round here looking for you this morning, but I told him you had left already." She smirked causing a chuckle out of Tasha.

"Yeah, well he must've known you were lying cause he found my ass..."

"Foreallll?" Pepper gushed while laughing.

"Um hmmm." Tasha nod her head. "But fuck that shit... come on."

"What you gon' do about Ralph's nasty ass?" Pepper asked. "Cause I came up with a plan... ion know if you gone be down but it can work."

Tasha stopped walking to check her friend out. "What?" She asked with a raised brow.

Pepper rubbed both hands together. "We gon' write a letter to his wife..."

Tasha liked that idea although she knew it was a big risk. "Aiight bet... I gotta run in the stores tonight to complete some orders. I owe a few people and it's some nice change. Gotta grab some Balenciaga sweaters and shit. After that... it's on." Tasha knew Balenciaga's was gon' be a hit cause not everybody in the hood knew what it was or had access to it, but since boosting is what she knows, it kept her hip on a lot of shit. It was 2001 and niggas was still stuck in the past. She knew once everybody started rocking the sweaters it would be a big hit.

Pepper smiled proudly of her idea. "Cool... meet me at the spot later." They hugged and parted ways once they reached their high school.

CHAPTER 3

*T*asha carefully roamed the store making sure to pop the security tags from the sweaters, all the while her nerves got the best of her knowing that shit was gonna be hot tonight. Only thing that worked in her favor was the store was packed and so there was no way one employee could just only focus on her. She had an order for five of these Balenciaga sweaters and if she didn't fulfill it that would cut into her reup money on some coke for one, and for two, nobody would want to do business with her anymore, and she couldn't have that either. If she didn't work prestigiously and carefully she could fuck up, and a fuck up was something she couldn't risk because she needed money to survive and pay her bills... no money meant no place to stay.

Her eyes scanned the room waiting to catch somebody slipping, she didn't care who it was... it could be anybody, all she needed to do was wait around for somebody to walk out the door and be stopped by the alarm. She'd use that opportunity to pass through like nothing happened cause since the shit would already be beeping; they'd be checking the person in front of her and not actually her. This was her routine whenever she went to stores that were hot for the night or the season depending on what she was trying to get.

Tasha placed her tiny-framed reading glasses back on her face. It wasn't shit wrong with her eye, but the look definitely helped, and she always made sure she looked like a straight up geek when she was going in the stores. Lying low, she calculated the price in her head. She had seven sweaters in total. Two of them were for her and Pepper, and the other five priced at $1,090 are the ones that was about to make her some dough. She bust those down half price by selling them at $545 a piece making her a profit of $2,725 and that was good enough for her. It was just her luck when the exotic looking white woman that looked to be in her mid-twenties hit the door. Tasha knew from one look at her that she was in for trouble as she carefully watched the girl hand picking little items and even looked at the same exact sweaters. Tasha was smart enough to know where all the security sensors on the clothes would be, especially cause those shits were all in the tags too, but white girl was fucking up bad only going for the main sensors.

It was her initial thought to mind her business but then she thought *'what the hell somebody had to teach me too'* she eased over to the girl who was paying her no mind. The closer Tasha got to her she could smell the cigarettes on her body. She had her blonde hair in a high ponytail, her lipstick was a very dark matte black and her clothes itself were all black. 'Big Mistake,' Tasha knew that the girl was definitely being watched cause she looked like she needed to be. "Hey… you're being watched." Tasha casually moved diligently around the girl as if she was still shopping. "And you're popping the tags wrong." She whispered to her.

Instead of white girl taking heed to what she was telling her, she sneered her nose at Tasha. "Mind your fucking business." She growled before blowing her bubble gum making it pop. Without shit else to say, Tasha shook her head and walked away knowing that white girl would be the one she followed behind when it was time to get out of here.

Beep! Beep! Beep! Beep!

The system went off as the two red lights flashed. The corny security guard stopped the white girl. "Ma'am we're gonna have to check your bags." He pulled her to the side giving Tasha easy access to slip out. When she made it out, from the corner vision of her eyes she could see the white girl getting searched. "Bitch should've listened." She thought to herself before running all the way to the bus stop so she can catch the city bus back to the projects.

By the time she made it back, everything in the projects was in an uproar as usual but tonight it just seemed like police were everywhere, always fucking with somebody. She rounded the corner holding her bag tightly before she ran into Pepper who was in front of her building waiting for her. "What took you so long?" Pepper asked always happy to see her friend. "I've already written this damn letter and every-thing." She held it up dangling it in Tasha's face. "Look." She beamed.

Tasha chuckled at Pepper and sat down on the bench pulling the sweater from the bag that was meant for Pepper. "Here... this one for you." She smiled watching Pepper's eyes light up. She knew that Pepper would be happy cause they didn't come from shit and everything they have, they appre-ciated it.

"Yoooo... this this is wild right here bitch! Thank you, thank you, thank you!" Pepper put it up to herself admiring it. Tasha smiled at her pretty, chocolate friend cause she not only had a beautiful face, she had a beautiful spirit too. "All the hoes gonna hate me now!"

"Bet..." Tasha cracked up. "But look, come with me to

drop this stuff off, get my money, and then we can handle business."

Tasha and Pepper walked around the projects dropping off the product until Tasha had managed to collect all of her money. As they made their way through the halls of Tasha's building they were stopped by a nigga named Tru who practically ran the projects and he was much older than them cause he was already twenty-one years old and out of school. Tru stood about 6'2 and was a smooth dark chocolate with pretty skin and a skinny-framed body. Only reason niggas was even scared of him is cause he was deadly with a Draco and he had proven that plenty of times.

"What up Tash... Pepper?" He nodded his head acknowledging them both as he watched the lil young tender he had been talking to walk away. "Ya'll comin' to my party tonight?"

The whole time he spoke, he eyeballed Pepper from head to toe and although Pepper acted like she didn't see him, she peeped gamed. "Party? What Party?" Tasha asked. "I didn't hear nothing about no party and if it's yours then ion wanna have no parts in it cause ya shit be wild and the police always come knock your shit in. I'm good."

"Awe come on now don't be like that... ya'll slide." He smiled showing his deep dimples and gold teeth.

Tasha nod her head, "Okay we will see." She let him know as they walked off.

"And Pepper! Bring yo lil fine ass too!" He yelled behind them.

"Girlllllll...." Pepper giggled while blushing as she and Tasha made it to Tasha's door. From the outside she could already tell it was quiet on the inside, cause normally it would sound like a catastrophe. And on top of that, it was a fucking eviction notice on the door.

"What the fuck?" Tasha mumbled embarrassed as she snatched it off. She dropped her head and sighed. No matter what kind of shit she took on to survive, she just couldn't get the weight of the world off of her shoulders. She felt a tightening in her chest cause she knew that this was about to be her problem, it wasn't the first time either. She felt Pepper place her hand on her shoulder.

"You ain't gotta be embarrassed in front of me Tasha, we come from the same struggles; and shit we get one of these on our door practically every other month."

Tasha made her way inside with Pepper following behind her. Her mama was sitting at the table forking through a bunch of envelopes, but for whatever odd reason nobody else was around besides her mama's boyfriend who sat on the couch looking at TV with a beer can in his hand. Tasha slammed the eviction notice on the table in front of her mama. Tasha looked exactly like Vashon, just a younger and prettier version cause at 42 years old life had truly run Vashon down. "What's this??" Tasha fumed. "I give you money faithfully to keep the bills in this place paid! DayDay them give you money too so why are we getting evicted?! Why do you owe these people $3,000? This is crazy!" She fussed like she was the mother. She knew better than to curse at her mama cause that's one thing she would never do. She never wanted to block her blessings by being that disrespectful.

Vashon looked up from the table with weary, but wild eyes. She lit up a cigarette and blew the smoke in her daughter's face. "Don't question me little girl... you just better have my money. Where's the money Tasha? Cause I know you got it lil girl! The projects know you a lil hoe... all you do is fuck all night... you better have some money!" She sat the cigarette in the tray and lunged at her daughter like a wild cat. "Give me the money!"

"Ahhh!" Tasha fell and hit her ass hard on the floor. She tried to cover her face from her mama putting any scratches on her but she knew this behavior all too well. Money coming up missing and her getting her ass kicked for no reason at all was a sign that her mama was back on that shit. "I didn't do shit! I don't have no money!" Tasha cried. She knew she could easily beat her mama but she refused to put hands on her. She was sick of this shit and she was tired of being forced to be an adult when all she wanted to be was a kid.

"Shut up bitch!" Vashon continued to assault her only daughter until Tasha's cousin DayDay came busting through the door to pull her off since Pepper didn't wanna touch Vashon and her lazy boyfriend wouldn't dare get involved. Tasha felt Vashon going in her coat pocket and she tried to stop her from pulling out the money but it was no use cause her mama was too quick. "Look at all this prostitute money!" She waved the money around with her hair all over the place.

Pepper shook her head going to help her friend up. "That's fucked up..." she hissed.

DayDay, who was just as confuse scratched his head while trying to get Vashon to calm down. "You need to chill the fuck out Vashon! The fuck you beating on the girl for, you wildin' and this exactly why I got a place with my girl and I'm out this bitch..."

Tasha stood up out of breath with a busted lip as she tried to catch her breath. "You...you can have it... you can... have... have all of it." Her chest heaved while she used the back of her coat sleeve to wipe the blood from her mouth. "She's back on that shit DayDay." She told her older cousin.

He simply looked down at Vashon and shook his head. "I'm goin' to pack me and my son shit, I'm out." He walked away. So did Tasha and Pepper, they walked in Tasha's room and closed the door.

"That's it!" Tasha cried. "That's all my fucking money from the sweaters man." She felt a pain in her chest as she flopped on the edge of the bed. "I have a couple of dollars left from last night but I can probably sell my birth control pills cause all the lil girls who don't want they mama's to know they fucking be looking for them anyway. They come up with that money."

Pepper felt bad, her own situation was fucked up but it wasn't as bad as Tasha. What she admired about Tasha the most is that she's a hustler and she made a way out of no way to survive but she herself didn't have a hustling bone in her body. She had to depend on her mama for everything and that's only when she felt like doing. Her mama wasn't on drugs or no shit like that and she did work a lil job at the corner store, but it wasn't enough to take care of her family of six. They kept a little food in the house cause her mama still was able to get WIC for Pepper's little sister, she also had food stamps too. The lights were always off and the water was always cold but just like Tasha... her mama jumped on her occasionally too cause she took the stress of life out on her.

"We gon' figure this out..." Pepper assured her friend in deep thought. However, Tasha knew she didn't have time to just wait around and feel sorry. Hopping up from the bed, she wiped her eyes and walked over to her suitcase to pick out an outfit. She opted for a red and black pineapple Adidas outfit, which was a bodysuit with the matching shorts. Next, she pulled out her matching shoes, her bamboo styled earrings that had 'Tasha' going across the inside of the middle, and she grabbed her small Cuban link chain. "We going to Tru's party... fuck it. I'll be back, let me shower." She ran off and Pepper didn't question it. Whatever she wanted to do, she was down cause they had to have each other's backs.

While in the shower, Tasha cared nothing about the 2-minute rule while scrubbing her body. She had mixed emotions as the salty tears cascaded down her face running into her mouth mixed with the hot shower water. To everybody on the outside she was Tasha from the projects, the hustler, but on the inside she was simply a broken little girl that wanted to live a normal life. Most didn't know her real story, but one day she'd tell it and have a great testimony. "On God, Imma make it out this shit." She whispered and sighed while closing her eyes. She did the only other thing that gave her comfort, she sang. It started off as a slow melody, she hummed until her beautiful voice could be heard blaring through the door of her room and also outside the bathroom window.

"Love, so many people use your name in vain.
Love, those who have faith in you sometimes go astray.
Love, through all the ups and downs the joy and hurt.
Love, for better or worse I still will choose you first."

She sang one of Musiq Soulchild's classic hits so beautifully that she didn't realize that she had put on a show until she heard the claps coming from the other side of the open bathroom window.

Sucking her teeth, she opened her eyes and slammed the window down before hopping out and drying off to get dressed. Pepper was still in her room and the rest of the apartment was quiet. "That was beautiful Tasha."

"Thanks." She mumbled.

"I really think you should do the talent show at the 'Jackie Gleason Theater' coming up... it's some big money involved and a lot of exposure." Pepper suggested. Tasha had actually been thinking about that lately but she just didn't know how she would find the time and she didn't wanna risk being booed or overlooked. She just didn't think her heart could take that. It would be some good money, and singing was one of her biggest dreams; to one-day make it big is all she wanted.

22

"I'll think about it... I might." She replied nonchalantly looking at her busted lip in the mirror. She grabbed some Vaseline off her dresser and winced a little while applying it. After she grabbed her stuff she and Pepper were out the door in no time.

CHAPTER 4

"We should've never came to this party..."
Pepper smacked her teeth as she leaned up against the wall since Tru hadn't come over and talk to her yet.

"What's yo problem?" Tasha danced around with a cup of liquor in her hand. Pepper was almost positive that was her second cup and normally Tasha wouldn't drink at a party. It was only because of what was happening with her life that she thought she could drink the problems away. Pepper didn't answer. "Ohhh I see, you trippin' over Tru huh?" She teased.

Pepper rolled her eyes trying to muffle a chuckle. "Nah, it's not like I'm sweatin' that nigga or nun' like dat." They both eyeballed him for a minute while Tasha gave her a funny look. "Aiight... shittt maybe a lil bit." They high fived each other.

"I sold all those damn birth control pills." Tasha gulped the last little bit in the cup and tossed it. "Aye Tru! Let me get another one!" She slowly started to walk over to him.

Pepper stopped her. "Nah bitch that's enough, you don't need to be drinking like this Tasha."

"Well you don't tell me what to do Pepper." She sassed trying to hold back tears cause the liquor made her emotional as fuck.

"Yeah well I'm responsible for you since we came together."

"NO THE FUCK YOU'RE NOT!" Tasha found herself yelling over the music. Pepper balled her face up wanting to go off on Tasha but she knew it wasn't her and it was the shit she was drinking.

"Aye Aye... the fuck ya'll got goin' on over here? Lover's Quarrel?" Tru walked up smelling all-good draping his arm around Pepper's neck.

"Nah..." Pepper hissed, "she tripping... but where the food at?" She walked away with Tru leaving Tasha standing there.

"Yeah whatever!" She yelled behind them. "Go then!" Finding herself sitting in a chair in the corner, her head was spinning while she watched everybody around her dancing. Visions of the way her mama attacked her replayed in her mind over and over no matter how bad she tried to shake it and the liquor wasn't helping, it was only making it worse.

"Get up." She heard a familiar voice looking up into the face of QUA. Immediately hopping up she was happy to see him as she put her head into his chest and cried. As mad at her as he wanted to be, he just couldn't no more. Besides, he knew he wasn't perfect either. He indulged in all kind of shit with other girls that he knew Tasha wouldn't approve of. "I'm sorryyyy... I'm so sorry...." She cried.

QUA didn't know what to do, he only wished that she would talk to him and stop hiding whatever else was going on with her. Although only eighteen, he wanted to protect her from whatever she was hiding but the fact that he couldn't was making him feel like shit. "I'ma catch up with ya'll." He told the group of boys he was with; they'd just came off the block and was fresh into the party. Walking Tasha to an open bathroom he closed and locked her door. Sitting on the lid of the toilet, he sat her on his lap and wiped her tears. "Tasha, what's wrong man? What's goin' on wit' you?"

She took a deep breath and sighed. "QUA I don't wanna talk right now but I promise I will." She closed her eyes and slowly started removing his belt buckle. Although he wanted to stop her, he couldn't cause he knew he was just as weak for her. Both wrapped up in their own thoughts as she slowly rode his dick right there until they were both satisfied. Tasha's perky titties were still hanging out when they heard a commotion coming from the other side of the door. She hopped up quickly. "What's that?"

"Let me see…" He peak his head out of the door. "Fuck! It's a raid! It's the police." He rushed to flush the weed he had on him down the toilet.

"I knew this shit was gon' happen!" Tasha yelled and before she could say anything else the door was being bust down.

"Get out! Get out with your hands up!" Officer Ralph forcefully pushed her and QUA out of the bathroom and on to the floor where cuffs were being placed on them.

"Yo Unc! You ain't gotta be doing this shit right here! We ain't even do shit!" QUA yelled to Ralph. He didn't know why his uncle hated him so much. In his heart, he felt it was jealousy.

"No! You shut the fuck up! You don't gotta be doing this shit here Quajay!" He snarled looking at him in disgust. "Just another young black ass nigga… a product of your environment."

"Man fuck you…" QUA hissed. He was met with a swift kick to his mid-section.

Ralph watched his only nephew wince in pain. "Watch yo fucking mouth."

Once they were down, he whispered in Tasha's ear. "You missed our meeting." Smirking, he walked away back into the bathroom. "It's more drugs in here!" He yelled out.

Tasha's eyes bounced around the room searching for Pepper just in time to see her and Tru being hauled out and in no time, they were in the back of a paddy wagon. Once they were down at the station, she and QUA locked eyes and again there was that look; that look of disappointment that he couldn't save her. They were all separated until someone was able to pick them up. All of them except for Tasha.

They called her name in less than an hour to be released, after they questioned her over and over about whose drugs belonged to whom and who was who. Who's the head of this and who was responsible for that. "I don't know shit… ain't seen shit and I'm not telling shit. I'm not no fucking snitch now call my mama to get me out of here." She spat sobering up giving nothing besides attitude. After a while it was pointless.

Making her way to be release she had to stop and hold her breath when she heard Officer Ralph talking to his sergeant. "Yeah, her mother is sickly, she's a very close friend of the family. I'll make sure she gets home."

"I shouldn't be doing this because you're not a guardian Ralph. You know the rules." The white haired, dark skin man replied to him signing off on some paperwork for him.

"Hey man… a favor for a favor. I'll make sure the wife bakes you an extra sweet potato pie for the holidays this year." He grabbed his coat and stared at Tasha. He wasn't sure exactly what his infatuation with her was. He knew that he was wrong

27

but in his eyes Tasha didn't carry herself like a child... she was beautiful but a true product of the ghetto, a project rat. He'd been unhappy in his marriage for years and at 40 years old divorce wasn't an option because he had too much to lose and it was cheaper to keep her. Tasha thought she was a sex slave, but to him she was much more than that. What started off as a blackmail slowly turned into a strong lust, and somewhere deep down inside a deep care. He lay next to his wife at night while thinking about Tasha... a child. He wanted to stop this but every time he tried he couldn't find the urge. He wanted to just take care of her now, not be looked at with hate in her eyes for him.

"You hungry?" He asked as she sat silently in his patrol car while he drove back to the projects. She didn't say shit to him, just stared blankly out the window. "I just helped you out, the least you can do is say thank you Tasha." He told her in frustration with his deep voice.

"Thanks." She mumbled dryly wishing he'd just shut the fuck up and let her out but one look at him and she knew what he wanted, she knew what he was about to do, especially since they didn't pull up to the projects, they pulled up to "the spot."

"What happened to your lip? Did Quajay hit you?" He questioned taking his finger trying to brush it over her lip. Flinching, she pulled away from him. "I'm not gon' hurt you."

She shook her head staring out the window trying to fight back tears. "How much longer you gonna use me? What if QUA finds out?"

"QUA can't do shit for you, including keeping your ass outta jail." It pissed him off that she even brought him up. She knew that was the rule. QUA should never come up.

She sucked her teeth.

Being that she was on her ass broke again, she knew she'd be on the block heavy, which meant she needed him in order to not get caught. Swallowing the lump in her throat she looked from the building and then back to him before he got out slowly following behind.

Since she still had juices of QUA on her from the party earlier, she was forced to wipe herself down with an old rag and some wipes before laying her body on the dusty mattress where she closed her eyes and became his playground.

CHAPTER 5

"*A*rghhhh!" Tasha leaned over the toilet with her head sunken down in toilet bowl, while draping both her arms over the sides. Sweat perspired down her face, as the smooth, warm liquid made its way from the pit of her stomach before flying out of her mouth.

Pepper paced the other side of the bathroom door in a panic. "Yo what's wrong with you Tasha? You've been throwing up for weeks now. What's wrong?" She frowned with worry wrinkles in her forehead hearing the sounds of the door unlock alarming her to go ahead and walk in. Tasha was sprawled out on the floor as Pepper ran to her side. "Shit girl... you look a damn mess! You better not have been trying none of them drugs you sell or else I'll beat ya ass myself."

The more Pepper spoke, the worse Tasha's headache got. She felt Pepper was talking nonsense cause she knew damn well Tasha would never try no shit like that. She was right about one thing though, she'd indeed been throwing up for weeks and hadn't seen her period in two months. She was just scared to take a damn test cause she didn't want to have to face that reality. She was in no position to be having a baby and even risking not knowing who the baby's father was.

"You should take a pregnancy test or something… it's either that or the drugs." Pepper insisted.

"It ain't no damn drugs!" Tasha hissed wiping her face.

"Aiight bet…." Pepper pulled out her phone dialing a number. "Hey Tru… um yeah.. I know I was supposed to been called you back but something came up. I got you… I promise." She rolled her eyes. "Listen, I need you to bring a pregnancy test to my house as soon as you can."

Tasha spun around and tried to grab her phone. "Bitch are you crazy?? He's gone tell QUA!" She whispered in her ear with her face balled up.

Pepper fell back and shook her head, "No he's not…" She assured her and continued talking to Tru. "Yeah, it's for me, who else would it be for? Don't act like the condom never broke on us before. I just want to be sure; okay see you in a minute."

Twenty minutes later, Tru was at Pepper's door with a test. "You gon' let me in?" He asked looking at her crazy. Hell, he wanted to know the results just as bad as her cause he wasn't ready for no damn kids.

"Un Un." She pushed him out. "My mama has already been tripping lately." She reached up kissing his lips before pushing him out locking the door. She was glad that he didn't put up much of a fight. When she turned around Tasha was staring at her crazy. "I know I know…" Pepper held up one hand walking pass her back in the bathroom. "I ain't even tell you I was even fucking him on the regular."

"You damn sho didn't… lil hoe." Tasha managed to chuckle as she snatched the test and opened it. Pepper leaned against the door. "You gonna watch me take the test Pepper?" She asked.

She nodded her head. "Um hmm, yep."

Tasha shook her head as she nervously unbuckled her pants and pulled her panties down. She did exactly as the instructions said and then patiently waited until the words "Positive" read on the test. "Oh shit... oh shit... fuck man... fuck!" She pulled strands of her bundles biting down on her bottom lip so hard she was sure she drew blood.

"What you gone do Tasha? And who baby you think it is?"

"Pepper, I don't even know. I don't know what I'm gon' do but I can't tell nobody."

"And how long you think that's gonna last before you start showing?" Pepper questioned looking at Tasha's flat belly. Nothing about her appearance even gave a sign she was pregnant. There was a pause before they were both distracted from the ringing of Pepper's phone. It was Tru. "Tru... it's fine... I'm fine, it came back negative." She assured him. "We good... I'll meet with you later aiight? Okay... bet."

Tasha tossed the test, washed her hands and grabbed her bag. "It's late... I gotta hit the block in a few."

"Maybe you should rest tonight." Pepper suggested.

She shook her head as she reached in her bag to make sure the tiny bags of crack were there. "Nah, I wish... I gotta make money to pay my half of bills and make sure I'm good. I'll catch you later." She put her Wilson bomber on and brought her hoodie up over her head.

By the time she got on the block it was still people everywhere as usual but that didn't stop her from doing her thing. Sitting on the bench with her hands in the jacket pockets, she remained aware of her surrounding but she truly didn't feel well knowing that she had to push that to the back of her mind and stay focused. "What you need?" She asked the crack head standing in front of her, one of her regulars. Skinny Nita had been on crack for years and looked a mess.

"You know..." She sniffed real jumpy as her eyes bounced around.

32

Tasha collected the money before giving her the product as she watched skinny Nita walk away with a look of disgust on her face. She promised she'd never even play around with that shit after witnessing first-hand what it did to people, especially her mama. She battled with herself everyday trying to figure out how to get off the block, but if she didn't make the money none of them would have a place to stay.

She looked around caring nothing about the young couple engrossed in a full fist fight in front of her, or the bad ass kids playing tag on the playground when they should've been in the building some damn where, nor did she care about the thugs or the lurkers. Her goal was one thing and that was the green. When she was all out of product, she got up ignoring a call from Ralph. Lately, she'd been igging him and she knew the shit would catch up with her but he'd been real weird, not only wanting her sex but wanting her time and she hated his ass.

Not risking getting robbed, she ran all the way to her building until she got to her door where she let herself in only to see her mama sprawled out on the couch strung the fuck out, and shit was everywhere. Her boyfriend lay next to her. Tasha wanted to throw the fuck up again as she walked to him using all the strength she had bringing her foot to his body with a swift kick. "This shit all your punk ass fault!" She hissed ready for a fight. He was so strung out he barely felt the shit, he couldn't move. She grabbed her bags and walked to her room closing her door.

Dropping the bags she grabbed a plastic bag off of her dresser and stuck her head in it, "Arghhh!!" She spit it all up trying to catch her breath. "Fuck! I don't have the stomach for this block shit no more!" She yelled to herself. It was literally even making her sick to her stomach. She decided she'd tell QUA everything, she was tired of being abused and hiding shit. Tired of being forced to be an adult, just fucking tired.

"QUA!" She yelled his name in the phone as soon as he answered. "Come to my apartment please. But don't come to the front door. Use the fire hydrant and come to the window." She told him before hanging up. Fuck it... she thought. She was going to tell him about the pregnancy and Ralph's bitch ass. Sitting on the bed, her body trembled as she wrapped her arms around herself waiting to face whatever may happen.

CHAPTER 6

*Q*UA had never heard Tasha so shaken up before, cause Tasha was tougher than any female he'd known and one thing she hated to do was show emotion. One of his biggest problems with her was she felt like she couldn't be weak around nobody, but hearing her admit she was pregnant and seeing the fear in her eyes had him spooked. Pacing her room he scratched his head thinking as he searched her huge almond shape eyes. "Damn... a baby Tasha?"

"Yes... a baby QUA... that's what I said and I'm not tryna do this shit alone. Hell, I wanna kill it!" She admitted. On the outside she was trying to be cool but on the inside she was trembling.

He wasn't trying to hear that. QUA was ready for his responsibility but he had one question. "Is it mine?"

Swallowing the lump in her throat she dropped her eyes. She thought she was ready to tell him the truth about everything but him being in her face made her realize she wasn't. How the fuck was she supposed to tell him that she was selling her soul for her freedom? Or that she spent most nights selling crack, or that she was even doing half the shit she was doing to survive. He knew the basic shit, not the extensive shit. Furthermore, how could she even tell him it was his own uncle she was letting use her body for his own motives? She just couldn't.

She looked him dead in his eyes when she told him, "Yes... it's yours. Why the fuck would you ask me something like that?"

He sat next to her wearing a Tommy Hilfiger outfit with the matching shoes as YSL cologne poured from his body dripping into her nostrils. "To be honest we ain't as close as we used to be and you be pullin' all kinda shit lately."

She sighed, cause she heard no lies. "I'm solid. I swear to you." she lied.

"So why you crying then T? Word is bond... I believe you." He wrapped his arms around her for a hug. "Don't kill the baby aiight? Lemme just figure some shit out."

She heard him, but her focus was on the big ass cockroach crawling on her ceiling threatening to fall on them both. *'I gotta get out this apartment'...* she thought to herself.... *'They won't even clean this muthafucka.'* She leaned up with QUA just in time to move him out the way as the roach plopped on her bed getting lost in the comforters.

"What happen?" He asked her looking around the room crazy.

She shook her head, "Nothing."

Boom! Boom! Boom!

"Tasha!" Her brother Eli yelled from the door. "Tasha!" He panicked and that wasn't like Eli to panic.

Swinging the door open she locked eyes with him. "What? What happen?" Her and Eli were a year apart, he was 17 and Cleo was the oldest... 19 years old and never around, only when he wanted to check on Tasha, but other than that

36

nobody saw Cleo. Eli's clothes were ripped and his dreads were wild. He was the male version of Tasha cause they looked just alike. Behind him, she heard commotion in the apartment and in the hallway. "What happen?"

"Come on man! Just come on! Somebody killed Cleo!" He told her out of breath before he took off.

She felt her heart drop to her ass. "Killed Cleo?" She ran out of the apartment and into the hallway and down the steps jumping off the stoop to get to the front of the building where everybody was running. She felt the adrenaline as she took off and she knew QUA wasn't far behind her cause she heard him calling for her. "Move! Move!" She cried pushing everybody out of the way. "Fucking MOVEEE!" She shoved her way through coming to a halt. There Cleo was on the ground with a hole to his chest as the crimson red blood seeped through his shirt. Lifeless. He was completely lifeless, yet peaceful looking. They'd had a rough life, which caused him to always wear this mug on his face but that was still her brother and she loved him. Caring nothing about the blood she ran to his side where she grabbed his hand. "Nooooo! Cleo Noooo! Get up baby! Please get up!!" She sobbed as everyone looked on shaking their heads and mumbling about what happen.

She felt QUA and Eli trying to lift her as she slapped them away with little clear snot trickling from her nose. "Don't touch meeee! Don't touch him either! Don't ever touch him!" She cried rocking back and forth. She whispered in his ear. "I should've told you I love you more. I should've called you more. We should've been way closer than we were... please don't go Cleo, let's start over." She whimpered and talk to him until QUA couldn't take no more lifting her off the ground cradling her like a baby.

"You don't need to be seeing this T... I'm sorry." He felt so bad he ain't know what to do. Tasha and the luck of her life kept him on a rollercoaster. He ain't know what to do at times. He looked at Eli who nodded his head of approval to take her away. "Get the fuck back! Don't ya'll see me trying to get through!"

Fucked up crooked ass police didn't budge while waiting for an ambulance, they didn't even seal off the scene cause this shit was funny to them! From the corner of her eye she saw Ralph approaching with a nonchalant, yet envious look on his face about the way QUA was carrying her. She jumped from his arms unexpectedly rushing at Ralph swinging. "Fuck you! Punk ass cops fuck youuu!! Ya'll see everything else around this motherfucker but ya'll don't see who the fuck is doing all this killing! Fuck you!!" She swung as he ducked catching her arms.

QUA grabbed him by the wrist. "Let her the fuck go... or I promise I'ma tell ya wife ya secret." He growled giving his uncle a look of death.

Ralph looked at his nephew like he'd lost his mind but he let him go. There was something in his eyes that Tasha saw. He was spooked by what QUA had just said. "You fucked up nephew, should've never did that." He walked off.

QUA watched him walk away while holding Tasha in a bear hug trying to hide her face from the scene. As he turned to go in her building her mama Vashon was walking out wearing a dingy house robe and a head full of rollers as she slurred with her words and talked shit trying to get to Cleo... but not a tear was in sight. Tasha wanted to punch her pathetic ass. Especially since she knew a funeral would be nonexistent since it wasn't no insurance policies.

QUA stayed with her and held her all night long with her room door locked allowing her to cry on his chest catching her tears. "QUA?" She whispered making sure he was up in the middle of the night.

"Yes T?"

"What was the secret you threatened Ralph about?"

He pulled her in closer. "Don't even worry about that... it's family business."

Instead of responding she lay there... this was the beginning of her depression.

CHAPTER 7

(2 months later)

Tasha sat in the doctor's office looking pale and uninterested. The past 2 months had been pure hell. She'd been depressed in the worst way. She woke up from Nightmares of Cleo lying dead on the ground that night. She was battling sleeping, she was battling with her weight cause she couldn't keep any food down, she had no energy, but still had to go to school and trap on the block without Ralph knowing. She vowed she would never give her body to him again after that night Cleo died. Seemed like he could clock everything else but where the fuck was he when her brother got killed? And the hood still wasn't talking; she couldn't even be mad cause that was the code and always had been. She could see her neighbor get shot right now and she wouldn't tell the police shit. Justice wasn't held in the court when it came to the hood; it was held in the streets. She had everyone in the projects labeling her as a clocker now... she didn't push shit, only watched the scene and they were willing to do whatever to make sure she was good cause she was genuinely good people.

QUA looked at her caramel brown skin as she sat waiting for the doctor to come in. Her mama Vashon sat across from them both not wanting to be bothered. She'd gotten so skinny she looked like a damn skeleton. Tasha was able to be seen at her first appointment cause Pepper's mama brought her being that she knew Dr. Dupoy very well but this time she had to bring her mama. The only way Tasha was able to get her to this appointment was by paying her to be here. Vashon truly didn't give a fuck about Tasha anymore. Tasha was everything she wanted to be... looks, street smarts, hustler... and everything. She hated her for that cause she couldn't relive her life and start over. Tasha thought she was grown in her eyes, and she no longer needed her.

Dr. Dupoy walked in holding some paperwork with a disturbing look on her face, nothing like the first time she saw her, she was all smiles. "Is everything okay?" Tasha asked her feeling something was off.

She cleared her throat, "Tasha, there's something I'd like to discuss with you but only if you'd like it to be discussed, if you'd like we can discuss it in private." She gave her a reassuring smile making Tasha even more nervous as her eyes bounced around.

Vashon stood up. "Shit, you ain't gotta put me out. I don't want to be here with ya fast ass anyway out there making babies and shit." She slammed the door.

QUA got up next. "Nah, don't go." She told him terrified by what the doctor wanted to tell her. She grabbed his hand but in no way could she had been prepared for what was about to come from Dr. Dupoy's mouth in regards to her HIV screening. *Positive... Positive...* she replayed those words in her head.

It took Tasha a minute to wrap what she was saying around her head but her mouth processed it before her brain did cause the room filled with her cries. Never in a million years did she think that she would be 16 and HIV positive. Never. It took the doctor and half of her staff to try to console Tasha while QUA boiled with both anger and fear. "Wait so what the fuck that mean? I got that shit too? That's what ya'll telling me?!" He yelled. Before they could make it to him he was punching the wall busting his own knuckles as the blood splattered. He knew damn well he couldn't have gave her that shit cause he wasn't reckless like that to be bringing her back shit. Her on the other hand, he knew something was off long ago and he shouldn't have trusted her.

"QUA pleaseee!" She trembled. "Please stop!" She begged long enough to grasp his attention. One look at her and he was leaping toward her trying to attack her but she was quick getting out of the way.

"What the hell?!" Vashon opened the door hearing the commotion confused as hell and ready to go. She was itching for her next high and they were wasting her time acting like some circus clowns. By the time the situation was under control the police were there and both QUA and Vashon were long gone leaving Tasha alone.

Dr. Dupoy gave her some prescriptions and some cards for a support group that she wanted her to join during this challenging time. She was able to calm her down long enough to explain the steps to try and keep her baby protected from contracting the virus as well. Her Medicaid also covered a case worker from the support group be available to visit Tasha on the regular to make sure she took her meds and for overall support cause she was going to need it.

Dr. Dupoy felt sorry for the young girl. She could tell just by her mother's attitude that Tasha had it rough but she was all too use to seeing young girls coming in and leaving with life changing results. She wanted to just hug them all.

* * *

Tasha walked the 30 minute walk from the doctor to the hood. Not that she had to, but she just needed some time. Time to think and process what was happening right now. The brisk evening air smacked the exposed parts of her skin causing her to shiver and wrap her arms around her body; the Miami weather was kind of cool for whatever reason. The streetlights were starting to flicker on, the corner stores were locking the doors only using their gated service windows. Dope boys were on the corners and rats raced from both sides of the junk field streets. She wanted to talk to QUA so bad but knowing his temper, she had to give him some time.

On the corner of MLK it was packed. Pepper was standing on the corner hugged up with Tru cause that's all the fuck she did now days and Tasha couldn't stand it cause Pepper was smoking now and hanging out with different girls. She was even dressing different since Tru was spending hella cash on her. She locked eyes with her friend and Pepper quickly walked across the street to catch up with Tasha. "Yo, what up Tash? Where the hell you been?" Pepper asked out of breath smelling like sweet melons mixed with weed.

"I been around." She shrugged her shoulders walking slowly. "You?"

Pepper sniffed. "Nah, you been distant for weeks now... don't hand me that." She sassed.

"It aint me, it's you... you been busy with Tru and I know how that shit is." She nodded her head in his direction for emphasis.

Pepper looked back and forth from Tru to Tasha, maybe Tasha was right and it made her sad on the inside. On the outside she smiled. "Cheer up baby... I gotta learn how to balance the two" her eyes roamed from Tasha's face to her stomach. "You got a pudge now too, look at you." She chuckled and sniffed.

"Yeah..." She replied dryly. "Why the fuck you keep sniffing Pepper? You got a cold?" Tasha searched her eyes knowing better, something was off.

Pepper looked like it was something she wanted to say but she played it off. "Oh, it's nothing... probably catching a cold." She looked back at Tru who was busy serving one of his customers. "Tru said tell you what's up too."

"Tell him I said what's good. Look, I gotta go aiight." She pulled Pepper in for a hug. She saw right through this shit. Tru was too fast for Pepper and Pepper was so into him she was willing to do anything to keep up. Tasha hugged her long and tight.

"Why you acting like you ain't gon' never see me again Tasha? It's okay." Pepper choked up and sucked up some tears.

Tasha's heart was hurting. "Well why you about to cry then?" She questioned her and spoke her mind. "Pepper... I like Tru, you know that we solid and been solid but I think he's too fast for you... you wanna go talk?"

Pepper shook her head backing away from Tasha and into the street. "I'm not no hustler like you Tasha. Mama put me out a few weeks ago. I gotta do what I gotta do..." She told her as a look of sadness overcame her. "I'll call you aiight? I love you."

Tasha stared out into the now dark street watching Pepper go. "Pepper!" She yelled behind her. She spun around looking at Tasha. "If anything ever happens to me... promise me you'll take care of my baby for me."

Pepper nodded her head. "Promise!" She yelled. "But aint nothing gone happen to you. You the strongest bitch I know!" With that, she disappeared back to the block and Tasha made her way home.

When she got inside, it was the same ole scene, except Eli was actually home in the kitchen trying to clean up. He was the only brother she had left now. "Sup Eli..." She spoke sadly.

He turned around with his cocoa eyes looking at his baby sis. His slender 6ft frame was perfectly ripped, long dreads were neat down his back. His fingers perfectly manicured. His dress code always up to par. Tasha always thought that Eli was gay, like an undercover gay or something like that. He had no kids, never wanted a wife and she never saw him with a girlfriend. It was like... he was just undercover with it but she didn't care, he was still a true thug at heart. "Ray Ray got locked up today." He informed her. "How's the baby?" He asked.

The baby was the last thing she wanted to talk about, and she damn sho didn't want to talk about Ray Ray cause he'd always been a fuck up, but she still gave an answer. "Okay, I guess. I'm tired, I'll see you tomorrow." She drag her feet walking away.

In her room behind closed doors, she made up her mind. She'd go find a job, she was done hugging the block.

CHAPTER 8

*M*oney was tight for Tasha and although it took her a few weeks to get there, she felt good when she filled out the application for McDonald's and they actually called her back. She knew it wouldn't be the fast money she was use to but she was willing to give it a try. She'd just worked her first shift and her feet were tired and her body was cramping. She was trying her best to cope with having HIV but she'd lost a dramatic amount of weight in the past few weeks from stress and worry. On top of that, she hadn't seen or heard from QUA… nobody had. Then again, she hadn't seen nobody, not even Pepper. She was still running up in stores when she had big orders but most of her days were spent hiding out in her room pretending to be sleep so her mama wouldn't fuck with her.

She changed her number from Ralph but she made sure to text QUA with the new number and still no reply. She beat the pavement up with her black work Nikes and her work uniform smelling like fried foods and grease. She carefully walked around a broken streetlight in front of the hood's corner store and when she looked up, there was Ralph riding along side of her in his street clothes and his brand new Cadillac Escalade. Her heart started beating fast as hell as the saliva built up in her mouth. If he wasn't such a pedophile he would be fine as hell, but she couldn't even look at him that way. All she could think about are the ways that he took advantage of her body and the nasty things he did to her.

"You been ignoring me huh? Freedom don't mean nothing no more? You must think clockers can't go to jail too Tasha." He slow drove on the side of her with one arm hanging from the window.

"Yeah well ion do none of that shit no more. I'm done with this shit. Don't you see this uniform? I'm legit now so fuck you." She hissed.

He ignored her statement. "Sorry about your brother… ole boy was a good dude."

"Don't you ever fucking bring him up. He's dead and buried. It's been over two months now so let him rest. What else you want with me?" She asked agitated ready to get this over with. She wanted to ask him about the HIV so bad but because she wasn't sure which one of them she contracted it from she couldn't say shit… at least not now anyway.

He looked at her with lust in his eyes until he noticed her stomach. Wrinkles appeared on the top of his forehead. "Um… nah, just wanted to make sure you was okay. Let me get goin'." He sped off down the street.

"Yeah! Run like a pussy now!" She yelled fighting back tears. She had already accepted she was gone be a single mother anyway. Fuck it.

She fast walked to her building and was hit with another surprise. There QUA was leaned up against the wall wearing a full black and white Nike sweat suit with the matching fitted cap. He twirled a black and mild in between his fingers as the night lights reflected onto his skin showing that he was relaxed and looked well rested. Tasha stopped in front of him not knowing what to expect. From the look in his eyes, he missed her, but he was hurt. "I heard you was working now, how's that going?"

"It was my first day today so I'll see..." She said shyly. "Just tryna do the right thing QUA." She sighed.

He slowly nodded his head and stared in her eyes. "Look, I should be mad at you but I can't stop from loving you. We need to talk..."

Her eyes bounced around as butterflies in her stomach arrived. "I... um.. ion know what to say QUA... I didn't mean to..."

He cut her off. "Tasha... I got tested. I'm not positive. I tested negative."

Her eyes flew open. "Wait what? You foreal?"

He nodded his head. "Yeah."

She didn't know how to feel, it was like mixed emotions. She'd been so depressed and that was one of the biggest weights on her chest. "So..so.. that means you couldn't have infected me then... but we.. like.. how? How are you not infected?"

"Ion know... that shit crazy but I don't have it. Gotta be God." He lit the black and mild and as quick as he did he put it out. "Secondhand smoke... my bad."

"Wow... that's.. I'm happy for you. I'm happy you are okay." She shift in deep thought. It was only one other person who could've infected her.

"Fuck all that Tasha... you need to talk to me and tell me... everything. Who you been with? Where you get this shit from?" She licked her lips and held her head down. "Listen, I have a doctor's appointment tomorrow. Meet me here in the morning to go with me and I'll explain everything then." She looked at him with hopeful eyes.

He agreed, "aiight, tomorrow... and no games Tasha. Dead ass."

"I promise... no games." There was a brief silence between them both at this time, like neither one of them knew how to break the awkward silence. "Can I have a hug at least? I can't infect you with a hug."

QUA didn't know what he should do at first but she was right. A hug couldn't infect him. He loved Tasha but he didn't know how to look at her past her disease cause in his eyes that's what she was now... a walking virus, an infection. Hesitantly, he wrapped his arms around her but he couldn't deny how good she felt in his arms. She appreciated him hugging her cause she'd been yearning for a hug for months, from somebody who loved her. "I still love you T." He assured her. She couldn't even respond cause somewhere in those words she heard a 'but'... a 'but' as in 'I still love you but we can never be together again' and it broke her heart.

It was hard for her to part ways from him but she did, and she made her way inside to a loud ass apartment. As soon as she walked through the door her mama was coming for her. "You gotta move outta here before you have that baby Tasha... can't no babies come up in here and nobody told ya fast ass to be out there fucking every Tom, Dick, and Harry so it ain't my problem." She fussed as she sat on the couch smoking a cigarette.

Tasha simply ignored her and walked to her room... she wanted to get the fuck out anyway. If she could pay bills here she could pay bills in her own spot. When she came out; she walk to the kitchen where it was a sink full of dishes. The roaches were everywhere and it was just nasty. Pots were still on the stove with food in it from days ago. Grits, from a week ago. Old food in the microwave and etc. and she was just sick of the bullshit. *I don't understand how a house full of grown muhfuckas can't clean up after themselves...* she thought.

She pulled the bleach from under the sink along with some Pine-sol. It took her nearly an hour to clean the dishes and wipe everything down. She sprayed the kitchen down with Raid too to try and maintain some of the bugs. She would hate for Summer to swallow one of them one day in her cup of juice or something. Although Tasha wasn't ready to be a mama; she felt this was showing her what kind of mama not to be to her child.

She worked up a little appetite by the time she was finish with all of that so she made her a buttery grilled cheese sandwich since all they had was bread, cheese, butter, and some water. If Tasha didn't put groceries in the house, it wouldn't be none. They always waited for her to do it. She waltz in her room and shut the door again. This time, her phone was blowing up and she didn't answer one call. Lately, she'd received multiple death threats from unidentified numbers and she was tired of it; she didn't even know why but she was sure she knew who was behind it though. At first she didn't give a fuck; but now it was starting to get downright annoying.

One thing she did do was think about getting a gun. She refused to be caught out there slipping. She knew who she needed to speak to and that was Tru... anything she needed in that aspect; he could surely get. Tru had all kinds of guns. The only issue was if he was willing to actually help her or not. Tru was wild, but he wasn't reckless like that and she knew this but it was worth a try.

CHAPTER 9

*T*he next morning the alarm was waking Tasha up. She had to miss school for this appointment but she was seriously considering dropping out cause it was becoming to be too much now. On top of that it wasn't easy being 5 ½ months pregnant and carrying around a baby the size of a small melon. She didn't understand what people thought was cute about being pregnant but she just couldn't adjust to it no matter how much she tried. She didn't have maternity clothes but she always made sure she was cute and kept herself up with what she did have, which was a bunch of stolen shit anyway. That was the upside of being a booster; all her shit was free.

After she was dressed, she made her way down the stairs thinking about the meeting she had with her case worker from the HIV support group that she had yet go to. She knew Mrs. Harris; the caseworker meant well but she was tired of having to answer a bunch of dumb ass questions. She hated having to tell her business... she often wanted to ask her *'lady, how would you feel if I pulled out a pen and paper and asked you all kinda dumb shit like 'can you read, write, and fucking talk too?'* But she always held her tongue and was respectful cause she knew she meant well. She hadn't told Vashon the truth about whom Mrs. Harris was, cause she felt it was none of her business. Mrs. Harris came around to make sure she was taking her meds and for moral support. She really just wanted to help her cope with this situation.

Tasha made her way down the stoop and in front of the building. She thought she was gonna have to call QUA, but to her surprise, QUA really was waiting already. "Good morning."

"Happy birthday." He passed her a card and a bag from the jewelry store.

She gasped as her hand flew up to her mouth embarrassed. "Oh shit…"

He shook his head, "What? Don't tell me you forgot your birthday?"

"I didddd…" She shook her head and grabbed the card and bag. "Thank you so much." She managed to smile. She had been going through so much she didn't even acknowledge her own birthday. "Damn, I'm 17 today." She opened the bag to see a cute XO gold and silver dust necklace. She loved it cause she had been wanting one of those for a minute now too. "Thank youuuu. I love it." She beamed.

"No problem… so try to cheer up a little bit." They walked side-by-side. "Come on, I'mma drive." He said casually.

"You got a car?" She asked confused. He cooley nod his head while bobbing to a brand new BMW; a white one with the black racecar stripe going around it. "This is nice."

"Thanks." He started it as the engine roared. On the way to Dr. Dupoy's he didn't say much to Tasha and she could tell he was still standoffish. She realized that he stayed away cause he couldn't control his temper. Had he come around any sooner he probably would've hurt her real bad and she was okay knowing that. Meanwhile, in QUA's head he was still contemplating about whether he should fuck her up or not. He clearly knew that she had to be cheating on him, it was very clear. When they arrived in front of the crème colored building with multiple suites, he asked her... "So you gon' tell me now?"

"I'm gonna tell you inside... and I want you to promise me that you'll just listen to me and try to hear me out... please. Understand why I did what I did and why this is happening." Her voice trembled. "I'm a victim, I'm not trying to ruin your life."

QUA was getting nervous as fuck by what she was saying but he was trying his best to hold his composure. "Aiight." He got out. They both walked in not knowing what the fate would be when they walked out.

* * *

"Dr. Dupoy..." Tasha said nervously. "I have something that I need to tell ya'll and I'm gonna tell you from beginning till the end." Please don't interrupt me she said feeling sick to the pit of her stomach. Not knowing the outcome was antagonizing her.

"What are you saying Tasha? Is everything okay?" She asked worriedly. "Everything at home okay?" She knew Tasha's mother wasn't the best mother and she was often concerned about her but without seeing any physical abuse she didn't want to make a report or assumptions. She never wanted to assist in a child being pulled away from home for things that could truly be fixed.

She dropped her eyes. "I know who infected me... just let me explain cause I owe this to not only ya'll but myself. I've been holding this in for a long time now and I want this off my back."

Tasha told QUA and her doctor the entire story of Ralph

and how he took advantage of her, blackmailed her, and infected her all at once. She admitted to QUA that she sold drugs even after she lied and said she wasn't. She admitted that she that she didn't know who the baby belonged to as well and she wanted to test QUA for paternity while she was still carrying her baby, not after. Dr. Dupoy had tears in her eyes. What she'd heard was beyond her, something she never expected. She'd heard plenty of stories from intercity kids but never one like this. Meanwhile, QUA sat in the chair in the corner with an expressionless look on his face as his left leg bounced uncontrollably. Tasha knew what that meant, he was up to no good and he wanted to do something crazy. "QUA!" She snapped him out of his thoughts. He looked at her. "I know we aren't together no more... but you all I got... so please..." She begged without finishing her sentence. He knew what she was getting at but he made up his mind already; when the time was right, he was gone kill his bitch ass uncle.

He knew Tasha wasn't lying cause it's true. Ralph did have HIV and he passed it to his wife too; from a prostitute he use to fuck with years ago and that's not all, he even had a baby with the girl and the wife didn't know about that. He knew his uncle did everything in his power to make sure she didn't find out cause if she left his ass she gets half of everything and that's what he didn't want.

"Tasha... I'm going to have to report this." Dr. Dupoy informed her. "Everything from this point on is going to move fast. I'm proud of you for being so brave... you're very strong and now it's time for some justice."

Tasha agreed as she patiently waited for the police to arrive. When they did, they took her to the station after calling her mama numerous of times who simply wouldn't answer. Tasha didn't care, she gave her report and did what she had to do, and the doctor was right. Everything was fast after that. She was determined to get her life back. The charges were filed and he'd have to be investigated and picked up on all charges. Tasha knew this day would one day come that's why she made sure she kept text messages and recorded conversations and she never told a soul: not even Pepper.

CHAPTER 10

"The news around here every other day! You done got that man locked up! All this controversy going on! You making my doorstep hot Tasha! And I don't need these people snooping around my goddamn door worried about what the fuck I'm doing!" Vashon went on and on. Tasha didn't even argue with her cause she was right but she wished that she would have some type of sympathy for her. Her niece Summer came running from the back room to look out the window.

"Go back." Tasha told her and sent her to watch cartoons.

Vashon wasn't done. "When you leaving here? When you moving out?" She stood behind Tasha looking at the news crew. The shit has been all over the news and she was tired of seeing Ralph's face plastered everywhere. Tasha even had to quit her job and stop going to school. The police did the best they could do to keep her name undisclosed due to the circumstances of her age but that only lasted for so long before the hood started buzzing. She wished she could get away. It wasn't even so much as the hood hounding her; it was the goddamn press that didn't let her family breath;

which was even more disrespectful cause she's a minor. *She's so dumb she doesn't even realize she can sue them for harassing me too...* Tasha thought... *nah all she care about is her fucking drugs, dumb ass.*

"I'm working on it..." She mumbled. She was counting her money in her head. She had managed to put up a few dollars from her store runs but her McDonald's checks were going to the bills. She rubbed her belly feeling her baby move while wishing she had a plan.

"You know.. for all this shit you putting me through, you could've at least sued the police agency or something... got us some damn money."

"Why didn't you sue them? You're the parent... I'm the minor." Tasha reminded her. "Oh wait, I forgot... you can't afford one." She mumbled. "Just like you can't afford shit else."

Vashon walked up on her daughter flailing her flimsy arms. "What did you say lil bitch? You got something to say to me? Cause if ya fast ass kept those legs closed we wouldn't even be having this discussion right now so I'd advise you to shut the fuck up before you get fucked up."

"Okay ma..." Tasha shook her head not even wanting to argue with her. It was no winning cause she'd keep going on and on. Tasha couldn't understand what made her so bitter. She only promised herself she'd never be like her. Vashon called her so many bitches and dick sucking hoes throughout the years the shit didn't even faze her no more nor hurt her feelings. She could give two fucks about her rants and nobody else in the apartment cared either. The sooner she realized that's how Tasha felt she'd stop running that fucking mouth.

Knock! Knock! Knock!

Vashon walked to the door to answer it. It was Pepper, she came strolling in looking a little different than the last time Tasha saw her. Today, she was dressed down in a Fila tennis skirt set and was dripping with gold jewelry. She casually walked over to Tasha who still stood at the window. "Why didn't you tell me all this was going on Tasha?"

She gave Pepper the 'really' look before responding. "I called you at least five times already and no answer or call back so how was I supposed to tell you?"

Pepper leaned into Tasha and sniffed as she used the back of her jacket to swipe it across her nose. "We should've just went to report this from the beginning." She whispered not wanting Vashon to hear her.

Tasha sucked her teeth, "Oh really? And tell them what? I'm a 16 year old drug dealer whose been forced to have sex with this cop to stay out of jail? So just tell them I sale drugs and was doing some prostitute shit huh Pepper?" She hissed staring back out the window. "You don't know shit."

"You right, maybe I don't know shit, but what I do know is you can't sit in this apartment hiding. So what you have HIV life goes on… you'll be fine."

Just the fact that Pepper mentioned the HIV had her pressed. "Not now aiight Pepper.. not now… and what you doin' with yaself lately anyway?"

She shrugged, "Not much… just doing me for now."

Tasha nod her head and looked at her friend. "Pepper, you gonna have to hurry up and get a grip on yaself before you end up just like one of these coke heads we be talking about…"

Pepper nod her head, "Yeah… I know." She replied in a low voice of sadness. "But look, I just wanted to check on you aiight? I'll check you later."

Just like that she was gone again. Tasha didn't know who to call but when she got a call from QUA in the middle of the night, she was relieved. "Wake up T…" he told her sounding stressed out. "I'm coming to get you so pack ya shit. It's too hot around there right now and you don't need to be stressing or being harassed."

She sat up in the bed rubbing her protruding belly. "I've been getting death threats too QUA."

"FROM WHO? I'll fuck they ass up!"

"I don't know…" she shrugged. "People. Ralph's fans that believes he's innocent I guess.

"Look, we may not be together, but I'm not bout to let nobody fuck wit'chu you, and dats on bro."

"I know…" She agreed.

"I'll be there in thirty minutes."

Tasha hurriedly got up and packed as fast as she could. She couldn't say she was too thrilled about going wherever QUA was taking her cause whenever they were in each other's presence it hurt her to see the way he looked at her. It wasn't the same. He was afraid of her and she could tell. Like, just looking at her would infect him or something.

She gathered all the daily pills she had to take, the money she had and all her clothes. She only left all of her old teddy bears for Summer. She walked to her bed and bent down to kiss the toddler on her cheek. "I love you." She whispered feeling bad about leaving her cause she was really the only one in the house who watched her and now since Cleo was dead she was fatherless. Her mama was all fucked up and locked up for fraud and she truly didn't care for Summer since Cleo left her about a year ago.

She wished she could take Summer but she knew she couldn't. She couldn't afford to do anything for her right now in her situation and she just prayed they actually took care of her. She knew Summer would be looking for her, but she made a promise she'd call and check on her when she could or whenever Vashon wasn't around.

QUA met her at the door wearing a simple all-white Nike fleece and the matching air forces. Around his neck was a big ass medallion and he smelled good. He couldn't even look Tasha in the face when he grabbed her bags from her to take them down. Tasha didn't say bye to anybody in the apartment… when it was all said and done, she just left feeling like nobody would be looking for her anyway.

CHAPTER 11

$\mathcal{T}$he apartment QUA had her set up in wasn't
extravagant, but it was way better than what she was
accustomed to and she was grateful. It was a one bedroom with
a tiny kitchen, dining, and living room with one bathroom.
Everything was fully furnished and there was always food in the
house. She'd been sitting in the apartment for weeks now
though, and QUA was never home, she spent most of her days
writing songs and singing them out loud while making her own
beats. Since the apartment was in the Heights, which is about 30
minutes from the Projects, she didn't really see anybody, but she
did have loyal clients who she ran in the stores for, they just had
to meet her at the store across the street from the apartment.

Some days, she felt too weak to get out of bed, and other
days she woke up in cold sweats or having nightmares. Ralph
was still locked up behind bars and it was starting to die
down a little bit but her biggest fear was him being released
and trying to do something to her. She felt like she was too
young to die but she was smart enough to know that he lost
everything; his wife, his life, his career, his family... and a

person like that was capable of anything. She knew he was in there losing his mind, she knew this cause she was on the outside and still about to lose hers.

Today was a rainy day so Tasha balled up on the couch watching television. From the outside, you couldn't even tell she had the virus. Her skin was glowing, her baby hairs were neat and slick with her long ponytail and she'd gained her weight back. She tried not to be sad, but she was lonely as fuck. She knew QUA wouldn't sit around her cause it hurt him to do so. He wouldn't even talk to her about what he was into now days cause he'd been getting a lot of money and he wanted her to have no parts of his business life. Most of all, she knew he had to be fucking somebody, she just didn't know who and wasn't her place to ask. They were more friends now than anything else cause an intimate life was nonexistent and she couldn't blame him... hell she didn't even want to be touched.

On top of everything else, they were especially on pins and needles waiting for the DNA results and it was driving her crazy so before she even worked up a headache, she tried to doze off and take a nap. Which was short-lived cause Pepper called right before she got a chance to snuggle in on the couch good. "You home?" Pepper rushed.

"Yeah... what's up?" She asked curiously cause Pepper hadn't called her much.

"Okay, I'm coming over there." She hung up before Tasha got the chance to even ask her how she was going to get there with no address. When she called Pepper back, she didn't answer but within the next 45 minutes she was knocking on the door.

As soon as Tasha opened it up Pepper rushed her with a hug. "I feel like I haven't seen you in forever." She gushed rubbing her belly. "Here I got all these bags for you." She kneeled down picking the bags up out the hallway. "It's some stuff for the baby."

As mad as Tasha wanted to be at Pepper for neglecting her in her time of need, she just couldn't be that mad, and although she had tons of baby shit that she had already went up in the stores and got; she was thankful. "Thank you." She smiled wobbling to put the bags in the room. When she came out Pepper was sitting on the couch rubbing her arms. "You cold?" Tasha asked. "I should really be slapping the shit out of you... you wanna chase your dick and done forgot all about your friend now you doing shit you shouldn't be doing Pepper."

"No" Pepper chuckled catching herself. "You got something to drink?"

Tasha fixed her a glass of lemonade and passed it to her before sitting down next to her. Before she could say a word, Pepper was gulping the juice down like she hadn't drank shit in days. "Damn." Tasha laughed. "You thirsty? You want some more?"

Pepper chuckled. "Nah I'm good. What up with you tho' Tasha? I came to check on you.. I miss you, I didn't come to be interrogated."

"Shit I miss you too. I be lonely as hell, but you know... you got ya relationship so I understand."

Pepper nod her head in agreement. "Yeah that's true but one thing I did that I said I'd never do is lose myself in a nigga. I'm only 17 and caught the fuck up." She sucked her teeth. "Like everything revolves around Tru now cause he takes care of me but I'm starting to get tired of that." She honestly spoke. She watched her mama get caught up in a man for years and completely lost herself. Pepper vowed that she'd never get caught up like that and she did; got caught up and in love with Tru till the point that she only wanted to be around him as much as possible.

Tasha sat and listened to what she was saying. "Yeah... I feel you, shit... that's why I had to do what I had to do to make sure I had money. Even now, I gotta keep me some money that actually belongs to me cause this shit is crazy. Nobody gonna love you and look out for you better than you can do yourself."

"Nah that ain't necessarily true though." Pepper's eyes bounced around the apartment. "Look what QUA did for you. He set you up real nice."

"It's cause we have history and we're friends before anything, but QUA don't fuck with me like that, trust me. I barely see QUA now days. He pays these bills but I still have my own money. He just wanted to get me out the hood from the humiliation and this is a good start. Nice area, it's quiet, I don't have to worry about going outside getting shot or robbed. I don't have to listen to my mama calling me all types of bitches, hoes, and prostitutes... or waking up to big ass roaches all over me...it's just better. I needed this."

"I feel you... have you spoke to your mom?" She asked Tasha. Pepper had recently saw Vashon and she was strung out on that shit bad. Walking around the projects trying to do anything to anybody for a hit. Shit was embarrassing but Pepper knew Tasha was already going through enough and she didn't want to share that information with her.

"Nope, and don't want to. I hope she goes to the hospital when it's time only cause I need her consent but other than that fuck her. I'm never going back."

"Did you find out what you having?" Pepper asked trying to change the subject.

"Nope not yet, and I kinda wanna just wait and see when I have the baby."

"Ya'll took a DNA?"

"Waiting for those results now."

65

"Good, good." Pepper sniffed and stood up. "Well, I gotta get back to the projects and go cook cause Tru's ass can eat."

Tasha furrowed her brows. "Have you been to school?"

"Barely… Tru takes up all my time."

That made Tasha stand to her feet. "Why?! Bitch one of us has to make it! If something happens to me you're supposed to have your shit together to make sure my baby is good. I don't want you to be fucked up!" She yelled.

Pepper squint her eyes. "Why you keep saying that shit?! This the second time you've said that to me. Nothing is gonna happen to you!"

Tasha's nostrils flared as her voice cracked. "I could die from this virus. I may not see my child turn 18 years old Pep… you don't understand how hard this is." She wiped a tear.

"No, you don't understand how hard this is for me to talk about with you. I don't want to think about my best friend in the whole world dying yo." She pulled Tasha in for a hug as they both shed tears on each other's shoulder.

QUA walked through the front door looking confused. "What happen?" He panicked looking at Tasha. "Everything aiight? You aiight?"

"Yeah…" She sniffed wiping her eyes. "I'm okay."

"What's up QUA?" Pepper spoke. "As you can see you give good directions cause I made it." She managed to smile.

"Yeah I see that, but now I done walked into some real sentimental shit and maybe I should go." He chuckled taking the bags of groceries to the kitchen.

"No… I'm leaving, I gotta get back. I'll see ya'll later." She rushed out of there.

"What was all that about?" QUA asked putting the stuff in the fridge and the freezer. "Pepper been weird as fuck lately."

Tasha took a seat at the barstool staring at him. "Girl stuff."

"I figured."

"QUA… why did you do this for me? Get me away from the projects?" What she really wanted him to say is cause he loved her, but she knew that probably wasn't going to happen right now.

"Cause… I told you I'd always look out for you if you need me and these one of those times." He replied closing the fridge and grabbing the keys. "Lock up, I'll be back." he walked out the door gone again. Just like any other time; he refused to give her eye contact and he never stayed longer than 30 minutes at a time.

Tasha was lonely again and now she wished Pepper had stayed longer.

CHAPTER 12

"*I*'m nine months already Dr. Dupoy, and my pelvic bone hurts, my back hurts. Everything just hurts and I'm tired. Just induce me already pleaseee." Tasha begged over the phone. These nine months had come by so quick and the only good news she had gotten so far was that the baby was indeed QUA's baby. She just prayed that her baby would come out healthy with no signs of the virus.

"We'll give it another 24 hours and see what happens Tasha. I try to avoid induction unless it's a medical reason, which it's not. Just try to get some rest right now because you'll need it." She assured her. "Has QUA been taking his preventative medications?"

"Yes… he takes them although there's nothing to prevent. We don't do anything with each other. We aren't together." She reminded her.

"Oh… I see… hmmm… well again, try to relax and page me if you need me."

"Will do."

Tasha hung up not feeling any better and staying in the house only made her keep eating everything in sight. On top of that QUA was still always gone and she found out why weeks ago. He was hustling and entertaining whoever this new chick was he met from Scott's Projects on the other side of town.

She decided to go shower and make herself comfortable, but soon after showering and putting on her tights and t-shirt, she felt a gush of warm fluid trickling down her legs. "Holy fuck…" she mumbled trying not to panic. Calmly, she walked in the room to grab her bag and sat it by the front door. Next, she called QUA.

"Hello?" A female answered his cell phone.

Had the circumstances been any different Tasha would've snapped cause she knew her name showed up on his caller I.D and chick was just being messy as fuck answering his phone. "May I speak to QUA?" She asked through gritted teeth trying to ignore the mild contractions coming along.

"QUA! QUA! Ya baby mama calling!" She said with much attitude. Everything went silent for a minute and Tasha tried hard to listen to the muffles coming from the other side but from what she could hear QUA was snapping.

"Hello?" He finally got on the phone. "You aiight?" He ask concerned.

"My water broke QUA."

"Shit! Aiight stay put I'm on my way. I'mma call Vashon to meet us there so she can sign the paperwork and shit… just sit down.. don't move cause we don't need the baby falling out just keep it in there." He rushed off the phone.

As much as pain she was in she sat on the couch in laughter. That had truly made her day cause she knew he was serious. She had prepared for this moment for nine months and now that it was happening, she hoped she could face it.

* * *

Six weeks later, Tasha sat in the house looking at her sleeping baby girl in a bassinet looking exactly like the perfect mixture of her and QUA. She had a head full of beautiful jet black hair. Her soft skin was the color of cocoa and she had the longest lashes Tasha had seen on any baby. Tasha loved her baby so much and so did QUA. They were both genuinely happy when they got the results from the HIV test and Lyric didn't have it… she tested negative but she'd still have to be tested numerous of times throughout her life as she grew up.

QUA was staying home more since Lyric's arrival as well. He didn't want to do anything besides work, come home, and spoil her even when she was sleep he'd just sit there holding her. "You still up?" He asked her causing her to jump. She was so wrapped up into her own thoughts that she didn't even hear him come through the door.

"Yeah," she smiled. "I still can't believe I've got a baby."

"Yep… Tasha's got a baby." He sat down on the bed drinking from a plastic cup. Tasha noticed that he didn't drink out of glasses that she'd use, nor did he eat off the forks, he ate off of plastic everything. She couldn't blame him. He was afraid and if the shoe was on the other foot she would've been too. They didn't educate them on this shit and everything they'd heard about the virus prior to her condition was a bunch of fucked up shit.

"But Tasha barely got a brain." She mimicked the line from Tupac's song 'Brenda's got a baby.'

QUA chuckled. "Tasha gone be aiight cause Tasha smart as hell and you can overcome anything."

"I'm going back to school to get my GED and I need a job too. I've been thinking about this."

"I'm with whatever you wanna do."

"Foreal QUA?" She smiled with bright eyes.

"Haven't I proved myself enough?" He questioned.

"You have…" She agreed.

"What's on your mind?" He asked noticing the shift of her facial muscles going from relaxed to perplexed.

"Something is wrong with me… a lot of times I'm terrified thinking about if Ralph ever gets out what's gonna happen… he's trying to make bond. On top of that the trial is set almost a year from now and I'll still have to face him… and then… there's me; I can't be sure but I think I'm suffering from postpartum depression or something."

"Fuck Ralph you don't have to worry about him… and post what?" He raised a brow.

"I've been searching online trying to browse my symptoms and it's real weird. It's like some days I'm so drained and depressed I can't even get out of bed. Some days, I don't want to be a mom… something is happening with me and it scares me. Some days I don't even have an appetite, and as much as I love Lyric… some days I'm having difficulty bonding with her."

A look of worry appeared on his face. "So you feel like you wanna hurt her at times? Or yourself?"

She violently shook her head. "That's not what I'm saying. What I'm saying is… something is wrong and it's making me feel crazy. I don't want to bottle it up anymore. I've been thinking about calling the doctor. Maybe she can prescribe me some antidepressants or something."

"Yeah…" He furrowed his brows. "Do that." He said slowly. "And just know, I got ya'll."

"But do you still love me?" She asked. "I know I did a lot of fucked up shit and kept secrets."

"I aint no saint either so we don't even gotta talk about that shit. Of course I still love you T."

"But you're scared of me…"

He sighed. "I'm just learning how to deal with this new situation the best I can."

"You don't drink after me or nothing. It's like you think you'll be infected just from the smallest shit. You won't even sleep in the bed with me."

"That's cause I never been educated on how to deal with somebody who has HIV Tasha." He let her know swiping his hand down his face taking a deep breath. "This shit is hard for me. Most young niggas my age would've left by now. I'm still here. I'm taking preventatives every day. I gotta get tested every 6 months behind this to make sure I'm good. It's shit I'm battling too T."

Listening to him admit that had her feeling crazy but at least he was honest. "Can we go to one of those support classes? I want to try it if you don't mind. I'm not asking you to go as my man. I'm asking as my friend. Just so we can ask as many questions as we need to."

He slowly nod his head. "Set it up... I'll go." Tasha was surprised to hear him agree but she was happy as fuck as she hopped up to hug him. He hugged her back but when she kissed his cheek he froze. That made her feel fucked up but she wouldn't let it get to her. "QUA it's okay... it's just a cheek kiss and nothing can happen to you. I take good care of myself as well and do everything I'm told."

"I'm sorry about that... I just... man ion know." He shook his head.

"I understand, it's okay." She assured him.

For the rest of the night they tended to Lyric, watched a movie together, and QUA even fell asleep in the bed with her making sure to stay on his side. The next day was QUA's birthday and the three of them spent the day together. It wasn't a beginning, it was just a start.

CHAPTER 13

eeks had gone by and besides Tasha's postpartum depression, other things had been on the upside with her and QUA. The HIV support groups were a big help to them and it helped QUA to understand a little more instead of looking at her like an infected animal. It helped the communication with them a little more and it was all good until Pepper called one day.

"I haven't seen you! Where have you been Pepper?" Tasha fussed while filling out job applications that wouldn't require a diploma. She also signed up for a GED class during the day so QUA could keep Lyric and then go do his thing at night. The antidepressants were helping a little but she was trying her hardest to beat the depression.

"I'm in rehab Tasha." Pepper told her dryly as she started crying. "Rehab yo... can you fucking believe this shit. I don't wanna be a victim Tasha. I don't wanna be. I brought myself here in order to catch it before it gets too bad but ion wanna be a crack head... I don't." She sobbed.

Tasha stood to her feet while pacing with the phone. "You damn right you not gone be no crack head round here

sucking dick for a hit! You so much better than this Pepper...
you so much better. You just gotta be strong!"

"I'm not strong like you Tasha... I never have been yo.
This is crazy but I'm trying."

"Tell me the truth... did Tru lace you?" Tasha quizzed
vowing that she'd go back to the hood and fuck him up.

"No... God no... he honestly didn't... it was all on me.
He's not even talking to me right now unless I finish this
program. He said he doesn't want a crack bitch for a wife."

"Wife?" Tasha furrowed her brows.

"Yeah..." She sniffed her tears away. "He proposed to me
too, I'm gonna be his wife one day."

"Well I'll be damned..." Tasha blurted barely above a
whisper. "Congratulations on that."

"Thank you... thank you."

"I'm gonna try to visit you if I can okay? And just handle
up Pep... you can do it okay?" She gave her some reassuring
words. "I love you."

"I love you too." She hung up.

* * *

QUA CAME RUSHING through the door once again at the same
time while Tasha was feeding the hungry baby.

"Yo mama called."

"Yeah, well I don't know what for."

"Talk to her..."

"Fuck her." She hissed. "Guess what? Pepper's in rehab."

QUA tossed his jacket on the arm of the couch and
washed his hands before picking up the baby. "Hey mama."
He cooed ignoring a call from his phone. Whoever it was
called right back. "Look, I told you I was coming to spend
some time with my daughter aiight? Stop blowing my shit
up cause you don't even want shit..." he frowned as he

listened to whatever the response was. "What? Ion need yo permission bout shit and don't gotta explain to you what's going on under my roof. You knew my situation so if it's too much for you then bounce." He let the caller know after hanging up.

Tasha stared at the computer in her own world trying to act unfazed but it bothered the shit out of her that she could never have a normal life again, she was too scared to have sex again too cause she didn't want to risk passing the shit on whether she used protection or not. It was just a lot to deal with in general but she was trying. "Girl problems huh? I'll beat the bitch up if you need me to." She teased trying to make light of the situation.

"Nah…" He chuckled. "I'm sorry about that. Muhfuckas just get on my damn nerves. Give'em an inch they think they run you and shit."

"Nobody told you to go get you a girl though QUA… you know what comes with it." She let him now.

"Yeah well… you wasn't like that."

She shrugged. "Everybody ain't me."

She could tell she was making him think cause it was all over his face. "You right about that." He mumbled. QUA was truly torn and just as fucked up as Tasha. The hardest thing for him to do was not be with the one girl he truly wanted and that was Tasha. He was glad he shared a baby with her and was able to see her everyday whenever he wanted but the fact that he couldn't have the relationship he wanted with her tore him apart. "And Pepper… yeah I heard from Tru."

She spun around grilling him. "So why you aint tell me?"

"Cause T… you've got enough shit going on right now. You dealing with your situation, your depression, and being a new mommy. You can't worry about everybody else problems."

She swallowed hard cause she couldn't even argue that.

"You know what I think? I think I need to get out of this house... something I haven't did in a long ass time."

"How about when Pepper comes back ya'll can hang out and celebrate?" He suggested.

Tilting her head to the side, she stared at him. "How about you take me somewhere until then?"

"And whose gone watch the baby? I'm not leaving her with just anybody."

"Yeah... you got a point." She exhaled hard standing up disappointed. "I'm gonna go shower."

In the shower, Tasha cried. She was afraid to tell QUA she'd been having suicide thoughts off and on, she was just afraid period. On top of that, bonding time with Lyric was getting worse. It was so on and off it was driving her crazy. Sometimes it was easy and most times it was just... hard.

Stepping out of the shower, she wrapped the towel around her and walked into the room where she stood in front of the mirror allowing the towel to fall forming a puddle around her feet. She examined her body cause it had changed so much right in front of her eyes. She was still a nice size but it was the new tiger looking stretch marks on her stomach that were now a part of her. "I'm only 17 ½ with a body marked the fuck up. I'll never be perfect again." She said aloud to herself.

"But you're still beautiful." QUA told her scaring the shit out of her. Her hands flew up to her breast as she covered them. "I've seen all that already." He laughed.

"QUA... get out! Now!" She fussed too embarrassed with cheeks as red as a beet right now. He was still laughing as he grabbed a pamper and wipes before walking out. She stayed in the room for a long time after that and after a while, she smelled the aroma of food coming from the kitchen... at the same time, Lyric was crying.

When Tasha walked out, Lyric was in her swing but

fussing to get out. She looked from QUA to Lyric. From Lyric to QUA. He was busy frying something over the stove and noticed her hesitation. "Tasha... you can fight this shit. I see how hard it is for you sometime but you got it." He encouraged her. She nodded her head and slowly walked to Lyric picking her up from the bouncer as she rocked her and sat on the couch until she was quiet. "See... she wanted her mommy that's all." He told her.

Tasha didn't reply, just stared at her innocent baby and hoped that when she got older she turned out nothing like her. She did the shit she did by choice but she was going to make sure that Lyric didn't have to be put in positions to do the shit she did. When she was good and sleeping, she placed her in the bassinet and sat at the table to eat the fried chicken, mashed potatoes, and string beans that QUA whipped up, which was so good and the first time she ever had his cooking. It was so good it put her to sleep after, but when she woke up in the middle of the night... QUA wasn't gone again like he would normally be. He was right there on daddy duty and she loved him for that.

CHAPTER 14

$\mathcal{T}$asha and QUA had been getting real close again it was her 18th birthday. She didn't know what she was going to do but she did start trying to get her life back. She was officially in her GED classes and when that was done she'd be able to work although QUA wanted her to stay home with Lyric who was now five months old.

QUA and her still weren't having sex but they were taking steps to get comfortable with each other even when it came to something as simple as kisses. It made her happy the times she'd see him online doing his own research on her situation in order to help them too. Today, he gave her some time to herself. He took Lyric while she got some much needed time to herself. She admired a cute ED Hardy outfit that he had copped for her and told her to wear tonight cause he was taking them somewhere as a family and she couldn't wait.

. . .

HE HAD EVEN WOKE her up to a brand new car this morning. It wasn't much but the two door Honda was good enough for her and she was grateful. There was only one problem and that was she didn't have her L's yet so she had that on the list to do. She still wasn't feeling herself but she felt better. Picking up her phone, she looked at the time and decided that she would catch the bus to the hood. She hadn't shown her face around there in forever and she did want to see Eli… and Summer too.

She knew QUA wouldn't be down with it but fuck it. She grabbed a hoodie and put it on over her clothes along with her favorite name plated Bamboo earrings and some Nikes. It didn't take no time to get there but as soon as she got off the bus, the air was different. In came a familiar smell of fried chicken, piss, and liquor. Bottles were cracked on the ground, there was more graffiti, and the clockers were out too. Bad ass kids ran around all over the place. She pulled her hoodie far over her head and tucked her hands in her army fatigue pockets as she made her way to her old building. She wasn't surprised to see an eviction notice on the door. Her heart pounded as she knocked on the door. She didn't want to be greeted by her mama and God answered her prayers. RayRay answered the door looking a damn mess. "Damn Tasha… long time no see." He let her in.

HER EYES ROAMED the apartment and it was a mess. "Where's Summer?" She asked.

"VASHON SENT her back with her mama when she got out of jail. Since you left it was never nobody to look out for her and you know I just got out too."

. . .

79

SHE SHOOK her head and slowly sat down on the chair watching the little tiny roaches scatter all over the kitchen counters and floor thinking maybe if they washed the dishes they could fix that problem. "Where's everybody else?"

HE SAT down across from her. "You haven't heard?"

"NO... HEARD WHAT?"

"VASHON HAD an episode so she's in the hospital... almost overdosed in this bitch, found her a couple of days ago strung out on the floor." He said shaking his head.

TASHA DIDN'T KNOW if she was supposed to feel bad or not, but she didn't, cause Vashon didn't give a fuck about her and never did. "And where's Eli?"

"SSSSS." He looked at her like she should've known what was going on around here. "I'll let him tell you if you see em."

"DAMN... THAT BAD?"

"YEAH... SHIT CRAZY."

SHE STOOD UP TO LEAVE. "Aiight... I'm out then."

. . .

"Heard you had a baby…"

"I did… a lil girl." She replied before walking to the door. "Take care of yaself RayRay."

"How is she?" He asked with a smile.

"She's good… lock the door."

"I got it." He answered before locking the door behind her.

Tasha never did really care for RayRay that much cause he was trouble and ain't have a lick of sense. Always locked up for some of the dumbest shit she'd ever heard of. He was definitely a special case and waste of good looks cause he was real cute but didn't know what to do with himself or how to carry himself. Him and DayDay were nothing alike and they came from the same wound; shared the same sac and you'd never know based of their personalities and lifestyles.

She wondered if she should call and check on Vashon; only for a brief second it slipped her mind and was gone that easy. Vashon ain't check on her and when she did call it was probably for some money. Tasha had been like a walking ATM for Vashon for years and she knew it too. The way Tasha looked at it was when Vashon put her out, it was her loss. She wanted her out so bad but still wanted her money and for the life of her she couldn't figure out how that shit was pose to work. Nothing like that would even hold up in court cause it was some straight bullshit.

WHEN SHE MADE it out and down the steps she had to hold back the tears. As soon as she rounded the corner she ran smack into Eli and couldn't believe what she was seeing. There was the only brother she had left on the stoop with a pipe to his mouth. His used to be neat dreads were all over the place. His lips were ashy as hell and he'd lost a ton of weight too. He didn't even realize she was standing there. She felt her lips trembling before anything came out of her mouth. "Eli?"

HIS BLOODSHOT EYES shot up at her as he smiled. "What up Tasha…" He spoke slowly. She couldn't say shit. "What? You ashamed now? You can't talk to a nigga no more? You left… you don't… give a fuck anyway."

THE TEARS SEEPED from the corners of her eyes without her approval. "I left cause I had to! Why you doing this to your-self? What you tryna do huh?"

HE PLACED his mouth back to the pipe for a second and then to her. He just looked… dirty. "Don't come round here judging me aiight? This is how shit is! My shit is fucked up and this is what it is and I'mma do what the fuck I wanna do…"

· · ·

"But.. but... Eli..." Her voice cracked as she examined him some more. Underneath his nails were even dirty and he would never have allowed that. His shoes were busted on the sides and he wore no socks. He looked like he had that same shit on for weeks... and he smelled bad, real bad.

"No! Don't judge me, just don't be like me, be better than me. You ain't like us Tasha... you ain't never been like us... get the fuck outta here, these projects toxic...."

She stood there frozen.

"GO!" His voice boomed so loud it scared her causing her to snap back to herself. She took one last look at him and took off running. "That's right little sister! Run!" She ran all the way to the bus stop with tears in her eyes. By the time she sat down her adrenaline was pumping so hard she had to catch her breath. She didn't even give a fuck about how people were looking at her. *Fuck them...* she thought to herself. They didn't know her or shit about her and if they did know her they better had sat there and shut the fuck up.

She was so glad to see QUA hadn't made it back home yet cause she didn't see his car but when she walked inside, it showed he had been there and left again. The little apartment was filled with pink and gold birthday balloons. There was decorations on the table, a food spread, and a three tier cake with her name on it encrusted across the top blinged out. Tasha was at a loss for words, it was so pretty. Nobody had ever did shit for her for her birthday; QUA always got her a nice gift but family wise she never had a birthday party or a cake, not ever.

SHE DIDN'T KNOW what his plan was but she literally had no time to do anything besides shower, style her hair, and get dressed. When she was done, he was walking through the door with Lyric in a rush. "Watch her... gotta get dressed." She did what he asked and pushed the thoughts of Eli to the side.

* * *

YOU CAN FIND me in St. Louis rolling on dubs,
  Smoking on dubs in the club,
  Blowing up like Cocoa Puffs,
  Sipping bub, getting perved and getting dubbed,
  Daps and hugs, mean mugs and shoulder rubs.

NELLY'S LATEST HIT 'COUNTRY GRAMMAR' blared from the speakers. An hour later their tiny apartment was filled with people they had both known for years. A couple of people from the Projects and a couple of people just from around the way. He had put together an entire little party for her since she hadn't been able to get out and because they both would still be able to keep an eye on the baby. Tru was even in the building but nothing made her day more than to see Pepper walk in a few minutes after him looking well and healthy.

WITHOUT A WORD they both embraced each other. What was understood didn't need to be explained. In a matter of a year and a half, they'd watch so much shit change right before their eyes but they appreciated both the good and the bad. "I'm so happy to see you!" Tasha beamed. "I'm glad you okay."

"It was tough Tasha but I'm aiight ya know? I had to check myself and catch that shit. I was being a weak ass bitch to the very same shit I said I'd never do; was turning into a straight coke head."

Tasha waved her off. "We don't even have to talk about that. You're here now and that's all that matters."

"I know." She dropped her eyes.

"What?" Tasha questioned. "What is it?"

"I saw Eli..."

"Yeah... me too..." She shook her head. "But we can talk about that later. Let's go party and play some cards."

For the rest of the night they danced and had a good time mingling and talking to everybody. They ate until they got full, they sang until their voices were almost gone, they kicked ass in cards and took everybody's money too. QUA was having a good time just watching her enjoy herself but Tasha could tell it was something on his mind cause she knew him, however, she was going to find out later cause now wasn't the time.

PEPPER AND TASHA hit all the latest dance moves and some old too. They shared a few lights drinks and laughed so hard their stomach's hurt. They had worked up a good appetite and ate chicken wings, meatballs, sweet pork-n-beans cooked the hood way with extra sugar and potato salad too. Even QUA was happy to see her happy. She had that sparkle in her eyes again. The strongest girl he knew. He knew one night wouldn't get her back to normal but he felt like it was a start.

HIS PHONE RANG all night from different girls that he'd been cutting off and he wasn't even interested in talking to nobody either. Sure, he had plenty of sex throughout the last few months but none of it meant nothing. Sex was just sex, especially cause he wasn't trying go there with Tasha just yet. He wasn't ready and wanted to take all precautions. However, he knew in due time it'll all fall in place. He walked away for a second to go and check on Lyric. She was fine in her bed sleeping like the music wasn't even bothering her at all and that's cause they trained her to sleep through noise. The house was never super quiet, a TV, radio, or something was always on for this reason. They didn't want noise to bother her or wake her up.

A COUPLE of hours later and everybody was tipsy and full, When they sang happy birthday, QUA stood behind her holding her by the waist. "Make a wish." He whispered in her ear. She closed her eyes and asked for God to help her and prayed all her demons off of her… eventually it'll get better. When she opened her eyes, she blew out the candle and this was the happiest she'd been in a long time.

BY THE END of the night, they were tired and exhausted. "I'm not cleaning all this up tonight." Tasha giggled flopping on the couch.

QUA SAT NEXT TO HER. "You so pretty." He told her with lazy eyes.

SHE REACHED up and kissed his lips… nothing too deep, just a peck, but to her surprise, he did more and actually kissed her… like passionately. Something he hadn't done in a long time. It felt like they were kissing all about five minutes before they came up for air. "Thank you…" her chest slowly heaved up and down.

"FOR WHAT?" He quizzed.

"FOR TRYING… for everything… even for going over and beyond to make me happy on some of my darkest days. I know one day, I'll be free from all of this."

HE PULLED a box from his pocket and opened it showing her a ring. "Give me your right hand…" he grabbed it and placed it on her ring finger. "This is a promise I'll always be here as

long as I have breath in my body. Don't ever forget that." He
told her.

SHE ADMIRED the ring and nod her head. It wasn't a big ring,
but it was beautiful and she'd cherish it forever. "I love it."
She beamed.

"GOOD..." He sighed. "So, I've been wanting to talk to you
about something but I just ain't wanna spook you."

"WHAT?" She frowned with worry wrinkles on her forehead.

"THE POLICE HAVE BEEN tryna keep quiet about this, but they
left Ralph out on bond."

HER HEART DROPPED. "He's gonna kill me QUA..." She leaned
back feeling a stabbing in her heart. "He lost everything
because of me."

"NAH, he lost everything cause of his muthafuckin' self and
cause he's a fuckin' pervert and he's not gon' fuck with you
or my daughter cause I'ma handle it."

"BY DOING WHAT?" She asked.

· · ·

88

"Just know… I got you it don't matter, he's not getting away with that shit."

Tasha didn't know what he was getting at but she knew he wasn't a killer. QUA could easily win a fight and had no problem checking niggas but he had never caught a body so that wasn't her concern. She was just afraid of him doing something that could get him taken away from her cause she didn't have nobody else. She felt alone, the little family she did have was done; that shit was over.

"Don't worry bout nothin' go get some rest." He told her.

Without another word, she stood up and walked into the bedroom where she grabbed the baby and for the first time allowed her to sleep with her in her bed.

CHAPTER 15

*T*asha and Qua had been inseparable in the upcoming weeks; the only time they were apart was when she went to GED class and he was in the streets hustling. Today he was taking them out to lunch but had to stop in the projects first. At first Tasha was hesitant but he did just like he said and was in and out. When he got back in the car he was all ready to go but Tasha stopped him. "Wait!"

"What happen?"

She grabbed a sleeping Lyric from her car seat and wrapped her with a zebra printed blanket before getting out. As soon as she felt the difference in the air a wave of sadness overcame her. "I want you to take this picture with me and Lyric, for memories. She was glad it was quiet out and she assumed cause it was kind of cool outside. Black people always wanted to stay in when it was cold. She walked to the stoop that connected to her old building and sat down. She wore her hair hanging with a red headband that her baby hairs lay perfectly around. She rocked her favorite bamboos with the Cuban link around her neck. Her choice of style was a red, white, and yellow Wilson jacket with the matching yellow shirt. A simple pair of dark blue jeans hugged her body and the red high top Chucks she wore complimented the red lipstick surrounding her perfect shaped lips.

In front of her, QUA held the little disposable camera to snap her picture. "You gone smile?" He asked.

She shook her head 'No'... with that, he snapped the picture for her before they left and went to get it printed out for her to keep. She actually printed a few copies but the picture told a story just from looking at her.

The rest of the day went by good and after lunch QUA needed to drop them off and go handle business. Tasha didn't mind though cause she needed to study. After getting Lyric settled, she made a pot of spaghetti for the night and then showered before pulling out her books. As soon as she sat down her phone was ringing but the number was unknown, like a private call. "Hello?" She answered. It was nothing, all she could hear was breathing. "Hello?"

They hung up and called right back.

"Hello?!" She snapped. Still nothing. "Stop ringing this fucking phone!" She hung up with her heart racing. She felt in her heart she knew who it was, but how? How would he even get her number? Immediately hopping up she checked the door making sure the top and bottom was locked and she check the windows as well. Peaking in on Lyric, she was in her swing calm; not sleep but she wasn't fussing. Tasha called Pepper. "Pep..."

"What's wrong?" She asked alert.

"It's him... I know it's him. Somebody keeps calling my phone and just breathing and hanging up."

"What?!" Pepper blurted.

"Yes... that's what I'm saying."

"You gone tell QUA?" She asked.

"Yes... no... I mean shit, ion know. Ion want him to get in no trouble."

"No more secrets, you better tell him." She warned.

"Okay… I'll call you back."

Tasha hung up and called QUA numerous of times without getting an answer and that pissed her off. He always answered his phone. He was either in the streets or with a bitch. She didn't have a choice but to relax and try to lay down before the headache she was forming got any worse. She knew QUA would one day have to see his uncle cause they were family; and she was hoping they could talk it out but knowing Ralph and his cockiness it would turn into so much more.

Tasha peaked in on Lyric one more time and before she knew it, she was dozing off. She didn't even hear her phone when QUA was calling her back.

CHAPTER 16

A few hours later in the wee hours of the morning, Tasha was startled by QUA busting through the front door with blood all over his clothes. He rushed right pass her on the couch and ran straight to the bathroom where he leaned over the toilet vomiting. He was sweating and distraught. Real bad. Tasha stood at the door shaking watching him. She didn't have to ask him what was wrong, she knew this all too well, she'd seen it happen to both Cleo and DayDay when they caught their first body... but the question was who?

He coughed uncontrollably trying to get it all out. "Ta...Tasha... Ta..."

"Shhhh." She told him as she kneeled down beside him pulling him in for a hug; the tears rolling down her face as her heart pounded out of her chest. She was scared for him, she knew what he'd done but why, and to who was what she wanted to know. She was smart enough to know now wasn't the time for all the questions. She helped him get out of his clothes in which she put in the tub and drowned with peroxide to get the blood out before she put them in the washer where she washed them twice. Next, she helped him into the tub to rinse off and then she cleaned the tub in peroxide.

Lyric had waken up by then so she had to settle her down and then tend back to QUA. He lay in the bed silent wearing his boxers and a ripped chest. He stared at the ceiling. "I just wanted to talk to him... that's it. He attacked me."

"Who QUA?" She ask. "Did anybody see you?"

"Ion know T... ion even know." He leaned over and kissed her. He kissed her so hard like he knew something she didn't know. Like he never wanted to let go. One kiss, just one and that's all it took and much to her surprise; Qua was pulling out a condom and they were having sex. Not just any sex, like real passionate sex and at first it hurt so badly because she felt like a born again virgin but once that surpassed, she was able to be what he needed her to be... comfort.

Laying on top of her he ran his hands up and down her smooth thighs as she spread them even further bucking her hips to match his rhythm. QUA ran his tongue around her nipples devouring them like little Hershey kisses. No words needed to be spoken between them. They spoke to each other with their bodies. "I love you Tasha..." He told her in between kisses. "I love you and Lyric so much."

"Ohhh... we love you too QUA." She panted wanting to savor the feeling that he was giving her forever. Tasha was trying to focus but from the outside, she thought she heard noises around the window. Closing her eyes she focused back on QUA as he stroked her deeply.

"Cum for me Tasha..." He whispered in her ear. "Cum for me baby."

Squeezing her eyes tight. She released all of her juices. "Ohhhh I'm cummingggg!" She squealed.

"Mmmm me too!" He ejaculated his semen into the

barrier in between them. They both collapsed in each other's arms where they fell asleep.

In the wee hours of the morning, QUA woke up to clean himself off and slip on some boxers and basketball shorts. His head was hurting real bad, pounding uncontrollably but when he heard something on the side of the window, he knew he wasn't tripping. Cautiously, he walked to the window barely touching the blinds, just enough for him to see. His heart dropped when he saw the apartment complex surrounded with SWAT. Right then and there, he knew who they were there for. He fucked up, somebody snitched.

He had to think fast cause he knew if he didn't go out they were gonna eventually find their way in and find anyway reason to shoot his ass down and he couldn't afford that with both his girls in the house. Like a man, with his chest out and head held high, he laced up his Jordan's and shook Tasha to wake up. "Wake up T."

"Huh? What happen?" She popped up noticing he was dressed. "Where you going?"

"SWAT is outside, I know they here for me and ion want them to just bust in here aiight. I gotta go.. and I may be gone for a little minute."

She burst out crying with fear and panic. "QUA what did you do? What did you DO?!"

"I'ma be aiight T... I'mma try to beat this case with self-defense. You know where all the money is at, you don't have nothing to worry about. Just use my phone to call my lawyer. I love you." He kissed her and looked over to Lyric with sad eyes knowing he wasn't going to see her for a while... possibly a long time and it hurt him to his heart. He wished he could rewind the time cause he would've handled himself differently but what's done is done.

Watching him walk out of the apartment, Tasha would

never forget the look on his face as she held the sheets up to her. "I love you QUA..." were her last words to him.

Even when they had him cuffed and arrested, they still ransack the apartment looking for a weapon but only came up empty. Tasha's heart broke into pieces.

* * *

THE NEXT MORNING, Tasha made sure she got her baby settled and tried her hardest to clean up the place. Turning on the News; she was going crazy waiting for QUA to call. She patiently waited in front of the TV to see what stories were going to come up but when Ralph's picture flashed the screen followed by QUA's mug shot; everything went silent. She didn't even have to hear the story to know what happened. She grabbed her ringing phone. "Hello?"

"Girl what the fuck going on with bro? This shit is crazy his face is all over the news!" Pepper went off on the other side of the receiver.

"I'm trying to find out now."

Tru snatched the phone from Pepper. "Yo, if he did that shit, he's going down for capital murder. He killed a fucking cop who's waiting on trial for charges brought upon him dealing with you... not to mention that's his fuckin' uncle this shit crazy."

"Tru..." She sighed broken hearted. "I know... I know."

"Did you call his lawyer?"

"Calling now."

"Aiight do that, I'm on top of everything else."

When they hung up, that's what she did... called his lawyer, who was already on top of it. "What about the retainer fee?" She asked him.

"It's paid already... Quajay already put up for a rainy day. Don't you worry your pretty little self." Mr. Stern told her.

"This is going to be tough but I'm going to do my best." He assured her.

When she hung up, she knew there was nothing else she could do besides wait. Wait for another fucking heartbreak cause all her life had been filled with one disappointment after the other.

CHAPTER 17

onths had went by and they still hadn't released QUA; she hadn't even been able to see him cause he was in the hole. Locked down 23 hours and out for one hour of free time and that's it. Tasha had become miserable. She wasn't looking like herself anymore. She barely ate anything and her focus when it came to Lyric was almost nonexistent although she tried her best.

She was tired of complaining about her problems, she was tired of everything. She was too embarrassed to keep running to Pepper and Tru cause they were all now all she had. They had their own issues to deal with and it wasn't fair to keep calling cause she was depressed. She couldn't go out and do shit cause she didn't have a babysitter; no family; no help it was all on her. Her entire life had been thrown away. She sent QUA pictures of her and Lyric all the time to try and keep his spirits up.

At the end of the day though, she just felt like giving up. Lyric was about to turn one years old and she had nobody to celebrate with, meaning her father cause he should've been able to experience that. She was walking now and such a busy and happy baby. She was even more sad because Mr. Stern was supposed to call her today to let her know what the outcome was. QUA didn't want to go to trial, he decided against it cause they were going to try to hit him with a life sentence. Ralph's wife was the main witness. She was in the room all along when QUA confronted Ralph and he didn't even know. Apparently he didn't go to kill him, he went to talk and whatever happened he ended up shooting him right between the eyes and there was no denying the fact that he did indeed do it.

Hours had went by when the phone finally rang and Mr. Stern was calling her. "Any news?" She asked.

"Well… they've downgraded the charge from Capitol murder to 2nd degree murder, which still isn't good but at least we can try to cut that life sentence they wanted to throw at him. He's a good guy… he doesn't have any points and has only been arrested once before on a misdemeanor charge; so we're working on it. Try to stay put."

"Tell him I send my love…" She told him.

"Will do."

* * *

BOOM! BOOM! BOOM!

"Tasha open the door!" Pepper pound on the door. Tasha was in there knocked out and hadn't heard the door nor the phone.

"Wait!" She yelled with sleep still in her voice; she made her way to the door simply unlocking it and walking away laying back on the couch.

Pepper walked in with a frown on her face and nose turned up. "This place is a mess yo… and it stinks in here when is the last time you changed your garbage?"

Tasha shrugged. She really didn't want to hear Pepper's

mouth, she wanted to sleep. That's all she did now days, deep depression brought on nothing but sleep and no energy. "Lower your voice." She complained. Her hair was all over the place, and she was stink too.

"When is the last time you showered?" Pepper opened the windows. Lyric walked around with a shitty diaper on her and her unsnapped onesie was dirty too and she also looked like she hadn't had a bath, but still, she walked around playing and smiling just as happy. Tasha didn't answer her and Pepper shook her head. "Come on Tasha... get up yo. This aint even you. I've never seen you like this."

"Yeah well... when you been through what I been through you end up like this." She mumbled.

Pepper walked away and took Lyric with her. "I'm taking the baby... till you get yourself together."

Tasha hopped up grilling Pepper as her nostrils flared. "Pepper, if you take my kid out this house on God and everything I love I will fuck you up. You wanna be just like the rest of these muhfuckas... take everything away from me."

"Humph bet that got you up..." She shook her head. "Go wash your ass while I clean the baby up and clean this damn apartment." She told Tasha.

* * *

LATER ON THAT EVENING, Pepper was still there. She had cleaned up the entire apartment and even lit some candles to make it smell good. Lyric was clean and playing with toys. Tasha was clean and had even let Pepper style her hair in her traditional sleek ponytails and got her baby hairs back popping. When she was done with that, she cooked them a hot meal of lasagna, salad, and garlic bread but Tasha didn't really eat much; she mostly picked over her food but Lyric sat in her highchair eating everything.

Pepper didn't like how her friend was in a daze; she hated it and wasn't used to it. When she looked in her almond eyes before they were always bright and full of life no matter what she was going through; but as she sat across from her now, she didn't know what she saw… she would say… emptiness. All the life had been sucked right out of her.

She stayed for a couple more hours until Lyric fell asleep but then she had to go home and get herself together for work. She had officially started working at Wal-Mart and although Tru didn't agree with it, she was doing it for her. Pepper had never been independent about anything in her life. When she was living with her mama; her mama paid the bills, Tasha stole her clothes and made sure she had money in her pocket. Tasha fought her battles and kept her filled with confidence. When she got put out, it was Tru who took her in and supplied her with everything. She didn't know shit about taking care of herself so it felt good to go to work and make her own money.

When Tasha started getting tired, Pepper stood up and grabbed her things. "I'll be here tomorrow to check on you."

"Okay." Was all Tasha said as she threw the covers over her head on the couch. "Lock the bottom lock." She tossed and turned all night long after that. She had demons on her back riding her and the shit wouldn't stop. She wanted to scream. She woke up in the middle of the night in a cold sweat. The only thing she could do was drink a cold cup of water and go get in the bed. The clock read 3:25am.

For some odd reason. Eli ran across her mind prompting her to call him but she wasn't surprised when he didn't pick up. She only wanted to check on him, not wait until it was too late like she did with Cleo cause the time with him she could never get back. She looked at Lyric who was sleeping without a care in the world and she checked her pamper to see if she needed to be changed and she was fine so she lay there until she was able to fall back to sleep. An hour later she was right back up and going to lay back on the couch. She realized her condition was getting worse and she was now suffering from insomnia and she was suffering badly.

She had to pass by the bathroom to get to the living room and she caught a glance of all of her pills. She wished she could just toss them all down the toilet. Some days those pills made her so sick. It was just too many got damn pills to be taking in her opinion. She often wondered how long her life span really was but she was so tired of searching it up on the net looking for answers. "Fuck all this shit." She lay there mumbling until she was able to get some sleep.

CHAPTER 18

The morning came quickly and the only reason Tasha had the energy to get up was because Mr. Stern called with some news. "Tasha are you sitting down?" He asked.

Her heart immediately dropped as she scoot to the edge of the couch. "Just tell me."

"Well they had a private hearing this morning and he was sentenced." He paused. "He was sentenced to 50 years with the possibility of parole in 15 to 20."

Tasha felt a stabbing in her heart as she grabbed her chest rubbing it. She felt like she was having a heart attack. "Okay.. okay…" She whispered and hung up to catch her breath. What was all this for? She wondered. Why did God have to punish her? What had she done so bad in her past life to deserve this? If Tasha ever believed in God… on this day, this moment, June 7th, 2002 she no longer believed in God… or that anything good would ever happen to her for that matter.

She picked up her baby girl and held her for a long time watching the clock hit 3pm; that was what time Pepper got off. Tasha bathed Lyric and sang to her while she did so. "I want you to always remember my voice, I'll always be with you." She kissed the bouncy baby. Next, she fixed Lyric some scrambled eggs and sausage cutting the sausage up in little pieces. She played with her in the middle of the floor until she went to sleep and then she stared at her some more.

Tasha put Lyric in her playpen and then went to shower herself. She styled her hair the way she liked it. She lotion down real good, and she pulled out a pretty dress. When she was satisfied with her appearance she took her necklace off along with the ring QUA gave her; she attached the ring to the necklace and then placed then necklace around Lyric's neck. When she was done with that, she pulled out a piece of paper and sat at the table writing a note to both QUA, in which she stuck in the mailbox, and then one to Pepper, which she stuck inside of Lyric's playpen right next to her along with a picture. She then called Pepper, "where are you?"

"I'm like 15 minutes away, I'm coming. See you when I get there. I brought some stuff to make tacos." She told her before hanging up.

With a shattered heart and soul that was long gone, she grabbed a long belt from the closet and walked in the bathroom where she closed the door and hung herself. She was tired of hurting, she was tired of the pain, she was tired of living. Her entire childhood flashed before her eyes. Everything and everybody who hurt her came into play as her eyes rolled in the back of her head. Death was painful... but the other side was much better. In a matter of minutes everything was dark and Tasha took her last breath.

Tasha knew she'd probably hurt a lot of people with this one; including her daughter, but she could never be the person she needed her to be, she was too damaged and too much had happened. She was peaceful knowing that Lyric would surely be taken care of. The world was a better place without her and her misery.

* * *

Pepper

"This girl is really trippin' foreal." Pepper mumbled as she opened the door. "She left the damn door open."

Walking in the apartment it was really quiet. Too damn quiet for her but when she saw that Lyric was sleeping she was relieved. She put the bags down and leaned down to kiss her and that's when she saw the letter. *What the hell is this?* She thought to herself. "Tasha yo ass left the door open!" She yelled over her shoulder just as she started reading.

Dear Pepper,

First I wanna say I know you gon' be too mad at me when you read this, but I don't care cause there is nothing you can do about it. I just want you to know I love you so much. You've always been my sis. I've always looked out for you and I love how you looked out for me. A long time ago I always felt like this day was coming; I just simply didn't know how to cope. I lost everything... even my life cause technically the day I found out I had HIV is the day I truly died no matter how much I tried to cover it up. Remember I told you if anything ever happens to me that I want you to take care of my baby? Raise her with the love and care that I couldn't give her? Well now is the time; you got this baby... from the heavens to earth; I love you sis.. take care of you... and Lyric. Love always, Tasha.

Pepper's hands trembled as she finished the letter throwing it down on the floor. "TASHA! TASHA! WHERE YOU AT?!" She ran to the room and then the bathroom. Before she opened the door the tears were cascading down her face. There Tasha was hanging lifeless, skin turning purple and cold. Her eyes were closed and a pee puddle was beneath her. Pepper ran to her body trying to get her down. "NOOOO! Why Tasha! Whyyy?" She cried.

It took her a minute before she was even able to dial '911' or call Tru for that matter. She couldn't even watch them as they removed Tasha's body. She just couldn't. What she did know was she had to figure things out. It took an entire day for crime scene to take pictures and call child protective services. Because Pepper wasn't of kin they wouldn't let her take Lyric right away, however, she wasn't letting her be a product of the system; she just wasn't.

2 DAYS later

QUA opened the mail excited to see a letter from Tasha. He knew she'd gotten the news cause Mr. Stern had told him all about it. He missed her and Lyric like crazy and after finding out he was about to be transferred to Mississippi… some better news was good to him right now. Opening the letter, he read it.

Dear Qua,

I want you to know I love you so much and I always have. It amazes me how strong you are and how you keep your spirits up the best way you can while being in there dealing with the way they're treating you. Me on the other hand, I haven't been doing so well and I've truly put up a big fight the best I could. They say only the strong survive but I guess I just wasn't strong enough Qua, cause Lord knows I can't do this no more. I want you to know I appreciate everything you've done for me. I appreciate how you've stuck by my side and loved and protected me. I appreciate most of all how you remained 'you' and a man true to your words. Word is bond and you've proven that. This will be my last letter to you, my final wish is that you find happiness and peace and blessings. Make sure to always check up on Lyric and make sure when she's old enough she comes to visit you. Bars will never get in the way of you being a father and the way you two love each other is undeniable. Don't be too mad at me, just pray for me. Pray for eternal peace. From the heavens down to earth... I send my love. Love always, T.

QUA closed his eyes with a face soaked of tears. All he could see is her sweet face, that beautiful smile, the scent of her sweet body sprays and the last time they made love. He wanted to call home and find out was going on but he knew exactly what the letter was saying and he knew in his heart, she was gone. When he looked up, the warden was coming to his cell. Right then... he knew. Long live his Tasha, she would forever be in his heart and his life would never be the same. They knew not to even fuck with him after this news. His days became harder and his temper even came back. As soon as he got transferred he found himself in the hole once again for a nigga wanting to try his patience. The only thing kept him going now was Lyric, and the fact that he knew Tasha wouldn't want him to be acting out this way; he just couldn't help it. He lost his only true love and if he was home he felt like she would've never killed herself.

Tasha blamed herself for him being locked up and he blamed himself for not being there to stop her from doing that shit. Had he not gotten locked up she would've never went over the ledge when he knew for a fact she really couldn't take anything else on the heart. He just really couldn't control himself when he did what he did. He lost his temper and she took her life. That was something he knew he'd have to deal with forever. Even when he didn't want to face it.

CHAPTER 19

*P*epper couldn't fathom the thought of even having to bury her dear friend but she was thankful for Tru because he truly helped her and took care of everything. He even had a private funeral with nobody besides she and him there. Tasha looked so peaceful to her. Her makeup was perfect and her soft pink lipstick went well with her pink and white dress. They both shed a few tears standing next to her casket. The hood had been buzzing from the news of Tasha's death. They had even set up a memorial in front of her old building on the stoop where teddy bears and flowers swarmed the stoop. They had candles and cards and balloons too. See, Tasha thought she never mattered much to anybody but in reality she touched many people just for her being who she was and Pepper wished she could've saw that.

"Damn T baby… you fucked the hood up with this one." Tru shook his head just staring at her.

Pepper leaned into him as her tears fell. She was gonna miss her friend so much, she never had to live without Tasha. From the schoolhouse to the trap house, from diapers to panties, from girls to young women, they'd always been together. "Fly high Flyy girl... I'll love you forever." Pepper whispered. "You can rest now."

Her and Tru stayed a little longer before they walked out and went home. Pepper changed her clothes and looked around the one bedroom apartment thinking about Lyric. "We gotta get that baby." She plopped down next to him.

Tru knew this conversation was coming. He didn't know what to say cause he truly wasn't ready for any kids. "Not now Pep."

"Then when Tru? Cause time is running out." She went on. "With or without you; I'm getting her even if that means leaving you and getting my own place."

"You serious? You'd leave me?" He frowned.

"For her... in a heartbeat. Try me." She fold her arms across her chest. Kneeling down in front of him, she looked in his eyes. "Tell me what's the real problem Tru, why you making this so hard?"

Tru sighed taking a deep breath, he wasn't just this cold hearted nigga, he just had his own reasons and he saw she really wasn't gonna let this go. "It's not that I don't want to baby. I just ain't never been scared of shit in my life, not even death scares me. When it's my time it's my time... but being a father... that shits scares me like nothing else cause I've never had a father and the last thing I wanna do is fuck up at being one."

Pepper loved him even more for admitting that to her. "I'm glad you admitted that cause I was two seconds from walking out, but I do understand what you're saying. I want you to know you don't have to worry about what will come natural. If anything that will make you a better father cause you wouldn't want a child to experience what you did and I know you'd give Lyric the world. Instead of a fast 'no'... I'm just asking for a slow 'yes'... please bae, we can do this."

Just by the look in his eyes, she knew she had him and he was gonna come through. He took a long deep breath. "Aiight what we gotta do?"

She looked around. "First we need to move, into a house... no more projects. We need a two bedroom and she has to have her own things because CPS will check for that. I have a job and you have your landscape business to show your legit money. You don't have a record and neither do I... we can do it."

"Aiight..." he told her pulling out some money. "Here use this to get whatever she needs and find a place." He pulled out a little more money. "When you do, put that shit in your name. I don't want these crackers asking me all my business."

"I got you."

Within a week time, Pepper had found a place in a good neighborhood. A nice two-bedroom house that she deco-rated and put together the room for Lyric. She had to go through the courts and CPS to start the process to get Lyric but it was looking good so far. One last thing she needed to do was go to Tasha's apartment before they put a lock on the door and pack up her belongings. She didn't want to throw anything away. She wanted Lyric to have access to it when she got older and then she could decide what to do with it. In the meantime, it went to storage.

The hardest thing for her to do was be back in that apart-ment but Tru stayed by her side the entire time. She was so blessed to have him. She knew that QUA was blessed to even have a friend like him as well. They'd spoke to him a couple of times and he wasn't doing so well but he was hanging in there. They made a promise to him that Lyric was gon' be straight and they'd make sure of that.

* * *

THE DAY CAME when it was finally time for them to get Lyric and they couldn't be happier although they were nervous. It was a difference when you were visiting a child or a child was visiting you that you could give back to the mother or father, but this was a totally different ball game because she was now their full responsibility. Wouldn't be no going home to mommy or daddy. She would be with them full time. "You ready for this?" Tru asked Pepper.

She nodded her head. "Yep, it's only right. Time for us to grow up and get our shit together cause Lyric needs us. She's gon' have a much better life than we did."

Tru agreed as the case worker walked up with Lyric and her belongings. She was wearing a chain around her neck with Tasha's ring and this was the first time Pepper had noticed that. Lyric's eyes lit up when she saw them and she could tell the baby was happy to see some familiar faces, but her heart broke for her cause she knew one day all the questions about her mother were coming.

The first night didn't go so well. Lyric walked around cranky and fussy all night. No matter what they tried to do she just didn't want to be bothered. It's like she was looking for someone or somebody and was getting frustrated because she couldn't find them. "Tru I don't know what to do." Pepper sighed. At only eighteen, she didn't know what to do.

He sat on the couch watching TV. "She wants her mama bae… that's what she's looking for. I mean, I'm not no rocket scientist but it don't take one to kinda figure it out."

Pepper was starting to feel so bad cause she just wanted Lyric to be happy, then she had an idea. She ran to the trunk of her car and rumbled through the rest of the boxes that she had to take to storage until she found what she was looking for. "Bingo!" She rushed back in the house with a throw blan-

111

ket. It was Tasha's favorite blanket, the one she always used when she was lounging on the couch. It still smelled like her.

She picked Lyric up and lay her in her bed giving it another try but this time she put Tasha's blanket over her. As soon as she smelled that scent she immediately calmed down. The tears got slower and softer and next thing they knew, she was sleeping. Pepper snuggled up on the couch next to Tru where she soon fell asleep too. She never realized how much hard work it was being a parent, especially to a small child, but she was gonna get it together and she put that on her life. She didn't care what it took… and if she got it right; maybe one day she'd have a child of her own.

She prayed it would get better and it did. Days turned into weeks, weeks turned into months, and months turned into years. Before they knew it time had passed them by and a better time was ahead of them. Pepper went from a scared young lady to a praying woman.

CHAPTER 20 '17 YEARS LATER'

THE YEAR OF 2018

"*H*appy birthday to youuuu! Happy birthday to youuu! Happy birthday dear Lyric! Happy birthday to youuu!" The crowd chanted as they sang happy birthday on her 18th birthday. Lyric had her auntie Pepper to rent out a section of STK's Steakhouse on South Beach just for her little private party.

Her cake was beautiful and so was the minor decorations. She didn't care about being too flashy with everything, she wasn't hard to please and she truly enjoyed herself.

Pepper looked on and smiled at Lyric looking just like Tasha back in the day. She was the spitting image with just a little bit of QUA. Lyric had those beautiful cocoa colored almond shaped eyes with those long lashes. She had beautiful hair in which her baby hairs lay smoothly just like Tasha's. She was a little taller than Tasha was because she took QUA's height but she was slender with a little curves.

Lyric had taken Pepper and Tru through a lot of changes over the years and it wasn't easy but it was worth it. A lot of her ways were just like her parents, true hustler at the heart. Every time she would get in trouble for doing something... Pepper and Tru would have to sit her down and explain to her that her mother did those same things and exactly what the outcome was. It was like from all the stories Lyric was told about her mother... the more she wanted to be like her. It wasn't until her middle school years that she really slowed down and started taking life seriously.

She had everything a girl her age could possibly need. At 31 years old Pepper had done good for herself to make sure of that. She had managed to get her GED and also went to nursing school where she became a registered nurse working down at Miami Jackson Hospital. Tru wasn't too bad himself. He owned four mechanical shops and a landscape business but just like a true hood nigga at heart, he still dibbled and dabbled in the streets. In his eyes all money was good money.

"Auntie Pepper..." Tasha walked over to her laughing. "This lil get together is littttt."

"I'm glad you enjoying yourself with all your lil fast ass, wild ass friends." Pepper chuckled and pulled her close. "Come here... you see your friend Freda over there?"

Lyric bust out laughing. "It's Rita auntie... Rita."

"Whatever." She waved her off. "Well don't be like Rita... Rita a hoe, she's always in the emergency room with coochie problems." She shook her head and frowned.

Lyric's eyes got so big and she was too embarrassed like it was her. "OMGGG that's TMI."

"TMI? What's that?"

"Too much information auntie... you gone have to get with the program if you gone be hanging with us." She chuckled.

"Well whatever... just don't be like her or else your coochie gon' fall off and I'm gon' have to sew you on a new one." She warned her.

"What? Wowwwww." Lyric chuckled covering her mouth

knowing she'd never be able to look at Rita the same again. "I keep my coochie to myself."

"That's my girl." Pepper high fived her. In a way, it was like she was able to be a parent while still having a piece of Tasha's friendship through Lyric cause they were really close and Lyric acted just Tasha.

Lyric grabbed the chain with her mother's ring that was still around her neck. It was a habit to always make sure it was still there cause she never took it off. "Where's Uncle Tru?" She looked around.

"Right here..." He told her walking up looking clean as day. "You know I wouldn't miss this. Happy birthday baby girl." He kissed her cheek handing her a pair of keys to a baby beamer. Her eyes lit up.

"Noooo... you foreal? It's mine? Where is it?" She jumped up and down.

"Outside... the baby blue one... and it's a graduation present and a birthday present." He reminded her since she was graduating the upcoming weekend and had a full scholarship to Florida State University.

"Thank you! Thank you! Thank you!" She ran off with her friends to go look at it.

Pepper gave him a knowing look. "I already know... it's fully covered and everything. She gone be aiight bae." He kissed her lips. "We did okay... I'm proud of us."

"Me too..." She grabbed his hand walking to the table to finish eating.

Tru and Pepper had never had biological kids of their own and they never even tried. They truly dedicated all their time to Lyric. They even made sure they took her to visit QUA a few times a year and they too had a real good relationship.

When the party was over; they agreed to let Lyric go hang out with her friends as long as she promised to be responsible. Pepper always worried whenever Lyric was out doing something. She just didn't want her to ever get caught up or influenced by the streets like they did. Lyric had never been to the projects. She had never seen much of what life was like for them back then and Pepper always wanted to keep her away.

Tru on the other hand didn't agree. He felt like she should know her background but after years of debating, he just let Pepper have her way like he always did. Happy wife; happy life.

* * *

BY 3AM PEPPER was pacing the living room floor furious as hell, especially since Lyric hadn't answered not one phone call from her all night. She only responded via text saying it was too loud at the party they were at for her to answer the phone. Tru lay there on the couch just watching his beautiful wife about to pull her damn hair out. "Bae leave the girl alone, she aiight damn. She's not gon' do nothing crazy."

"No... I knew you shouldn't have got her that car. She's never stayed out this late."

Tru couldn't believe what he was hearing. "You're fucking with me right? You do remember what you were doing before you even turned 18 years old. It's her birthday Pep... she's fine."

"Yeah... whatever." She mumbled pulling out her phone to call her again. Still, no answer. She finally lay on the couch where she and Tru both dozed off. And hour later Lyric came stumbling through the door barely being able to walk and Pepper knew she'd been drinking. She hopped up. "Lyric! You done lost your damn mind walking in this house at 4 in the morning. On top of that you're fucking drunk! So you're drinking and driving?! How fucking irresponsible is that?!"

She held up one hand trying to make it to her room. "Please auntie… not now."

Pepper looked to Tru and grilled him. He was now up watching everything. "Leave her alone; let her sleep it off and I'll talk to her tomorrow."

"No you won't! You never handled shit…you always allowed her lil ass to get away with everything Tru! Now suppose she would've killed somebody or what if she would've ran herself off the road?" She tried to make him see where she was coming from.

"You're right." He agreed. "And like I said, I'll handle it when she sleeps it off cause right about now the girl can't hear shit you talking about and it ain't processing to her."

He stood up to check on her. She couldn't even make it in her bed, she was on the floor next to her bed snoring like a baby. "Humph… leave her ass right there too." Pepper fussed and turned to walk away. She was so damn angry she couldn't even get any sleep after that and Tru didn't either. He changed and went to work out in the garage.

A couple of hours later, Pepper was in the kitchen scrambling up some eggs and frying sausage with toast. Lyric came walking in with a bad hangover looking like shit. She sat at the barstool and lay her head on the island.

"You know I'm pissed with you right? How fucking irresponsible it that Lyric? Why would you do some shit like that and then not answer my calls?"

She didn't want to hear this shit this morning cause she wasn't in the mood but she answered anyway. "I was in a party."

Pepper snapped her head back. "And?"

"It was loud."

"And you thought it was okay to get drunk at this party?"

Lyric shrugged her shoulders. "Yes… no… I mean, ion

know. It just happened. We was celebrating, we're about to graduate and it was my birthday."

"It's nothing wrong with that Lyric, but you have to be smart at all times. That wasn't smart at all... now what if you would've hurt somebody on the road? You would've fucked up your life and somebody else's all for a drink? I see this shit at my job all the time Lyric... all the time."

Lyric, being young and naïve responded the best way she knew how. "Well it didn't happen that way so can we just leave it alone?"

"I swear your mama wouldn't have done no shit like that." Pepper hissed almost regretting what she said as soon as it slipped out.

Lyric's head shot up. "I don't know what my mama would have done cause you don't tell me nothing about how she really was! All you do is compare me to her like you hate me for not being her!" Lyric fumed. "Guess what auntie... I'm not Tasha! I'm Lyric! And every time I try to get to know Tasha you tell me I don't need to know the bad shit! I only need to know she loved me! I don't know how she got HIV! But what I do know is I've been getting tested once a year all my life until I was finally in the clear! I don't know where she lived! Where she came from! What she did for money or nothing! I don't even know myself cause I don't know where 'I' came from!"

"Lies! That's all lies! I've told you plenty of shit!" Pepper frowned.

"Yes! Good stuff!" Lyric reminded her.

"And bad too!" Pepper defended herself.

"No! Wrong! If I did something bad that was relatable to something my mama did 'THEN' you'd tell me about it. Other than that you haven't told me nothing! Nothing about my family or nobody! Seem like when ya'll buried my mama... ya'll buried my past and hers too!" She stood up to walk away.

Pepper felt like she had been punched in the gut. She had no idea that Lyric even felt this way. She thought she was simply protecting her from all the hurt of the past. She felt bad, real bad cause all she ever wanted to do was protect her. Tru had heard everything. He stood off to the side listening at first but now it was time for him to intervene.

He placed his hand on Lyric's shoulder. "Look Lyric, you was wrong last night and that's just the bottom line. I put my neck out there for you and told Pepper to leave you alone cause I felt like you were responsible and knew better. You can't argue something when you're wrong cause you can never fix a problem you don't acknowledge."

She calmed down a little listening from his perspective. Pepper couldn't believe it. Maybe her delivery was always a little more aggressive than Tru's but she was basically saying the same shit he was saying, only Lyric seemed to get him and not her. "I understand Uncle Tru... I'm sorry I put you in that position and it won't happen again." She apologized.

"Now... about all this other stuff. Is that truly how you feel?" He asked her.

She dropped her head. "I do feel like that. I don't know who I am, or the past. I don't even know what ya'll were really like before ya'll got me."

Pepper cleared her throat. "It's cause we never wanted you to be like us, we wanted you to be better and Tasha wanted the same thing."

"I'm my own woman now auntie. I can make my own decisions. You don't have to guard me to that extent, but I've felt lost cause I truly don't know. Like what happen to my grandparents... were they even close to my mom? Do I have any uncles? Cousins? It's just been me... me and ya'll and that bothers me. I need to know... it's not a want, it's a need."

"Have you ever talk to QUA about this?" Tru asked her.

She shook her head. "Nah, it's still too painful for him to talk about ma. I think it's painful for him to look at me cause I look so much like her. He never said it, but I sensed it plenty of times."

Tru felt bad for the girl. He walked away and came back with a box. "Come… sit.." he told her pulling out old pictures of him and Pepper from back in the day. "Let me tell you bout uncle Tru and auntie Pepper before we had to grow up. You may not wanna hear this, but I wasn't shit nice…" He started. He didn't hold back either, he told her their entire story and showed all the pictures for proof. Lyric couldn't believe it. She knew her uncle Tru was gangster but just seeing his old pictures, the way he dressed, him holding all type of guns and stuff really tickled her.

Pepper was kind of standoffish at first and not because she didn't want to be a part of their conversation, but because her feelings were hurt. She wondered, if Tasha were in this situation, what would she do? She asked herself that a lot throughout life. It only took her a few moments to figure it out, but she knew… she knew exactly what she had to do.

CHAPTER 21 'GRADUATION DAY'

*P*epper and Tru stood amongst the other guest in the crowd looking at all the graduates. They couldn't have been prouder of her for doing what they didn't do because none of them had walked the stage for a diploma. Not Tru, not Pepper, Tasha, or QUA. Somewhere down the line Tru and Pepper did get GED's in order to pursue careers and QUA even got his since he'd been locked up but Lyric was making them proud. Not only was she breaking the cycle. She was the first one to actually go away to college too and they knew it was because of the life they were able to give her. If she had to grow up in the projects like they did and be accustomed to surviving on her own, they were sure she wouldn't be on this stage today.

"Lyric Grace Anderson" they called her name to accept her diploma and cords and everyone clapped and cheered for her. Pepper even shed a few tears. Although she and Lyric still hadn't fully made up… she would never miss this day. She was truly a proud auntie and when she said she wanted to go away and study business and marketing; neither Tasha or Tru was surprised. It was in her blood to want to be an entrepreneur. They had a surprise for her and she didn't even know it.

After the ceremony they watched Lyric looking beautiful as ever taking pictures and shedding tears with her friends. It was a bittersweet day for them because they all were attending different Universities all over the country. They took Lyric out to eat to her favorite place; The Cheesecake factory and had all kind of gifts for her. She didn't even need to have a trunk party cause they had gotten everything she needed for her dorm as well. She was good and full when it was time to go but still, they had one more stop to go. "Where we at?" She asked when they pulled up in front of the Bus station. "What we doing here?"

Before she could say another word, when her eyes met his. The tears poured from her eyes with both shock and excitement. She hopped out the car and ran to his arms. "Daddyyyyyy!" She cried squeezing him tightly around the neck. Tru and Pepper got out the car watching letting them have a moment. Everything was right on time and perfect timing. They had found out a month ago that QUA was being granted parole. It took everything in them to hide it from Lyric, especially Pepper. She wanted to wake her up every day and tell her that her first true love was coming home.

QUA looked different now. The same, but different at the same time. His mid 30's were doing him real good. He gained some weight and was buff now. He still wore a low cut but now had a full beard. He was still handsome as ever. His heart skipped a beat as Lyric ran up to him; it was just like looking at Tasha back then; she was her twin and he still couldn't believe it. "What up baby girl? I love you sooo much... and I'm proud of you baby, you did it." His deep voice tickled her ear as he hugged her. QUA never liked to cry but this emotion was on a whole other level. He never stopped loving her and always thought about her. He had missed out on so many years and he never thought he'd see this day. He couldn't get back the time that was lost but he had a lot of making up to do.

"I loved you too daddy!" She cried. "I love you too! Welcome home."

They both walked hand and hand over to Tru and Pepper where they all smiled at each other. It was like a reunion like back in the day. It wasn't one dry eye and everybody was all smiles. QUA clapped Tru up and gave him a brotherly hug. "Thanks bro… for everything. It takes a solid man to step up and do what you did. I appreciate you foreal."

"I was scared as fuck back then but I wouldn't have had it no other way. We bro's and that's what bro's do." He nodded his head.

QUA then hugged Pepper. "You look good sis… I wanna thank you too. Foreal. I know Tasha looking down smiling on all us right now. This all she wanted; for everybody to be good… that's it."

Pepper choked up on tears. "I love you bro. Welcome home."

"Thank you." He smiled. "Anybody know what time it is?"

Lyric checked her watch and gave him the time. She was still in awe and she hoped he didn't have to go so soon, they had so much to catch up on. "Don't tell me you have to go right now." She whined.

"I gotta check in with my parole officer and the halfway house. I got a few hours to spare but I can't be late."

Pepper nod her head. "I got you. Where you wanna go first you hungry?"

"Nah… take me to see my baby." He told her.

Pepper knew that was coming because QUA never got a chance to tell her goodbye. He never got a chance to accept what happened.

At the gravesite... Pepper, Tru, and Lyric wanted to stay back and let him have his time. Lyric didn't like going there cause it always made her sad seeing her mama's name on that tombstone buried so young but when she watched from a distance watching QUA break down she started to cry as she fanned herself. "I've dealt with a lot of things but coming here seeing my mama like this... I can never deal with this shit." She sniffed. "It's just too much."

Tru and Pepper couldn't do anything besides console her. It was touchy for everybody.

QUA kneeled in front of the grave just looking. He read her name, her date of birth, the day she died. Yet, he still had a hard time accepting it. He tried to keep it together but before he knew it the tears were coming. This made it real for him to actually see it. "You fucked me up with this one baby..." He choked on tears. "I guess this is what it really is huh T? How you been up there? How's life on the other side? I knew you was hurting... I knew man." He sighed. "I tried to fix it all, God knows I did." For the next thirty minutes he talked to her and got it all out. When he stood up he felt much better. "I guess this really is goodbye T... take care of us baby. We love you." He kissed his two fingers and then placed them on her tombstone before walking away.

"You aiight bro?" Tru asked him. "Tru knew this was going to be an adjustment for QUA but he had his back with whatever he needed and that was a promise.

He nodded his head. "I feel a lil better... shit real now. It's just gone take some time." He admitted. The worse thing to do was see someone you love in the ground and never coming back, but what was even worse was not being able to say goodbye. Shit wasn't the same. You could never hear that voice. You could never see that face. You can't pick up the phone and call or none of that shit people don't think about. QUA knew, you had to love ya people while they were here cause tomorrow wasn't promised. He often thought about what life would be like had he hated Tasha for the shit that they went through? He was just glad that at that age back then he was mature enough to understand… it wasn't her fault. Just like many others, she too was a victim. Like most who the world knew nothing about.

"I feel you." Tru reasoned with him. He was glad that QUA was able to do this. This was the beginning of finally healing.

CHAPTER 22

The next stop was to a place that Lyric had never been to before but when she saw it her face got twisted up. Graffiti was all over the buildings. The streetlights were cracked and glass shattered on the ground. Litter filled the streets. Rats ran from each side of the street. Kids were playing on the playground. Rough looking boys were on the corners. When she stepped out the car it smelled like fried chicken, piss, and liquor.

"What the hell?" Lyric frowned. Where we at?" She was so unaware of this environment but Pepper, Tru, and QUA were all too familiar.

"This where it all started baby girl... this the slums. Betty B projects... where we grew up at." QUA told her.

Her eyes bulged. "Foreal? Ya'll grew up here?" Her eyes bounced around looking at everything. "I don't think I would've ever made it out here. I'd just die." She said. "It's so... so rough looking like OMGGG."

Pepper chuckled. "You wanted to know so bad... here you go. Your mama was living here when she got pregnant with you." Pepper pointed. "That was her building... 3rd floor."

"Wowww." Lyric said in awe.

"And that was my building when I was growing up, and when Tru and me first lived together that was our building over there." She pointed some more. "When Uncle Tru and your daddy used to hustle it was right over there on the corner." She pointed.

"Yep." QUA agreed. "Your mama used to be all over this place. She was one of the biggest boosters here... she kept everybody in all the flyest shit." He told his daughter. "Tru... Pepper... I wanna walk Lyric around and talk to her... give me a minute."

"Take ya time bro." Tru sat on one of the benches. It was sad to see some of the niggas he came up with still in the projects doing the same ass shit but it wasn't his problem. He was just glad he got out. Pepper sat next to him reminiscing. Despite everything else, they really did have some good times here.

QUA and Lyric walked around and all the old heads that remembered him was glad to see him... they were even more surprised to see Tasha's daughter and they had some real funny stories about her too. He showed her everything about where he came from, where 'they' came from.

When they got back in front of Tasha's old building, Lyric stopped him as she stared up to the third floor window wondering what the inside looked like. "You okay?" QUA asked her.

She smiled and nod her head. "Yeah, I'm okay."

"Anything you wanna know?"

She smiled. "Actually it is..."

"I'm listening." He replied curiously.

"Tell me all about my mama, the good and the bad. I wanna hear it all daddy... pleaseee." She begged.

He smiled at his baby girl looking like her mama's twin. "I guess I do owe you that huh?"

She nodded her head. "You do."

QUA knew he was a sucker for her already but he didn't mind. "Aiight, so her name was Tasha... and it went a little something like this..." He reminisced from day one and took her back to the beginning. It was their truth, her truth, and one thing was for sure; there would never be another Tasha.

The End!

A NOTE FROM THE AUTHOR

What's up ya'll. First I want to thank you all for supporting me with this release and throughout my journey. I wanted to give ya'll a book that was real and relatable. I discover that my creativeness goes to another place when I'm writing about things that I can relate to. Growing up in the hood, I've seen a lot of things. I've met a lot of victims. I knew a lot of Pepper's, Tru's, Qua's, and especially Tasha's. A lot of times people don't want to talk about HIV and how it affects people. They are afraid to talk about depression and how real it is but it is very real. I hope this story was able to touch someone somewhere. I hope that it was able to help someone. If you know someone suffering from depression, diseases, or anything else please help them get the proper help or counseling they may need. Everybody isn't as strong as 'a Tasha'. In this book she put a up a long hard fight but in the end, her fate would end up much different as we saw in this book. If you enjoyed this read... please tell a friend to tell a friend and also leave a review. Thank You- S.Yvonne.

SUBSCRIBE

For all updates... please subscribe to my mailing list by texting Syvonnepresents to 22828 and reply with your email.

Made in the USA
Coppell, TX
12 September 2024

37249125R00080